LIME CREEK

LIME
CREEK

Fiction

JOE HENRY

RANDOM HOUSE

NEW YORK

Published in the United States by Random House, an imprint of
The Random House Publishing Group, a division of
Random House, Inc., New York.

RANDOM HOUSE and colophon are registered
trademarks of Random House, Inc.

Portions of this work were originally published,
in somewhat different form, in *New Letters*.

LIBRARY OF CONGRESS CATALOGING-IN-PUBLICATION DATA
Henry, Joe.
Lime Creek: fiction / Joe Henry.
p.   cm.
ISBN 978-1-4000-6941-5
1. Fathers and sons—Fiction.   2. Brothers—Fiction.   3. Ranch life—
Wyoming—Fiction.   I. Title.
PS3608.E573L56 2011
813′.6—dc22   2010026779

Printed in the United States of America on acid-free paper

www.atrandom.com

Title page and part-title images © iStockphoto.com/© Stefan Ekernas

2 4 6 8 9 7 5 3 1

FIRST EDITION

for
Roscoe Lee Browne
and
Anthony Zerbe

. . . it is not the statistics that tells the story.
It is what went on in your heart.

—Mark Harris, *The Southpaw*

CONTENTS

I

II

I

ANGELS

She came on the train with her folks, Spencer says. For the waters. For the mineral hot springs in that part of the state. Her daddy suffered from the lumbago and in those days it was thought to be a cure. And too, the journey would be another facet of her education before she went back to one of those eastern girls' colleges. She was nineteen years old. Course I was young too, twenty, and fixing to go back to school myself. Which was my book learning, but I still knew the horses better than anything else.

And that summer I was breaking and starting the

3

roughstock on a great big spread at the foot of the Wind Rivers while my own folks were still busy with their hay back home, which was maybe sixty or seventy miles to the north. And you know I druther be bucking broncs than haybales any day that the sun comes up. I been able to talk sense to animals, especially the horses, since I was a boy. And in the early evenings when her folks'd retire before dinner, Elizabeth'd come out by herself and watch me working the unbroke creatures in the big corral.

The red disk of the sun is setting directly in my eyes whenever I look up from this lovely two-year-old bay colt that I'm working. And every so often he'll snort and tense and prepare to throw me away from him, with my left hand smoothing down his neck and my right arm resting over his withers. I keep talking to him rubbing softly up and down the bridge of his nose and he snorts again but still doesn't jump away because by then he already knows that he likes the sound of my voice.

And who knows how long I stand there like that, with my hands on him and speaking softly and all the while watching his eye and his ears. Which go from wanting to lie back and get away from me to coming forward again so he can hear what I've got to say. His brow lifts up real nervous-like and he snorts again with his eye

big and showing all its white, and then for whatever reason he glances at me one more time and looks away like
he's finally figured out that I'm not gonna be a danger to
him and so maybe he can ease down enough inside his
fear to allow how good my touch feels too.

It's full-on dusk and I'm still talking to him, rubbing
the corners of his mouth as I position myself where he
can look into my eyes whenever he wants to. But by now
I can see that he's decided that he can trust me. I always
carry this length of braided rawhide that my granddad'd
given me when I was a boy, and I take it out and let him
smell it and taste it too as I slowly move it past his teeth.
And then I make one turn with it around the back of his
lower jaw, Indian-fashion.

I rub his back down from his shoulder, talking all the
while and leaning against the barrel of his body with
more and more pressure until he's actually supporting
my full weight. He walks ahead a few steps with some
concern, because by now I'm pretty much hanging off
him with my arms across his back. He stops and I leave
my right arm over him holding both sides of the rawhide
rein snubbed up in my left hand, and without altering
the calm reassurance of what I've been telling him I slide
up and onto his back.

He locks his knees and starts to hump up his spine

and his ears begin to come back and then go forward again. He snorts and kind of bounces once or twice stiff-legged like that and then just relaxes and walks me over to the fence. Where Elizabeth is perched up on the top railing watching us with this funny expression on her face. Not hard but not smiling either. In a green sweater. I'll never forget that green . . . a green coat-sweater. Isn't that foolish after all these years?

Back across the dark, the clashing of the iron triangle calls everyone to come and eat, the hands at one long table and the foreman and his family and the guests of the ranch at another. Elizabeth walks a pace or two ahead of me as I come up behind her coiling my piece of rawhide. She turns when I get alongside and says, They always seem to trust you, don't they? And I say, Ma'm? And she says, The horses. They trust you because you don't try to trick them, do you?

It's too dark to see her eyes and I say, No'm, I just put myself in their place until we both seem to understand what the other's thinking. Well I think they're lucky, she says. And I say, Ma'm? And she says, The horses. I just think they're lucky. And as we approach the wide veranda I mumble mostly to myself I guess, Well I reckon I probably am too.

We don't really get to talk again for their stay is at an

end the following morning and they're bound back east. And in a few days I'm headed home myself and then back to school too. In Cambridge. In Massachusetts of all places. And as they say, the die seems to've already been cast without me understanding or even being aware of the wheels that'd been set in motion a long time before I looked up like that squinting into the setting sun and probably smelling not unlike the dust and rank horsehide of my then present occupation. For I'll soon be taking my own train ride. In the same direction too. And I remember my father and me leaving a little after three in the morning for Cheyenne, where the railhead's at.

My last night home, my ma comes in while I'm still packing and sits on my bed watching me choosing from the stack of clean clothes she's brought that're all folded perfectly like a pile of books, but soft and warm from her ironing. And without looking up, as I'm arranging everything in my case the way I want it, I say, You know I met a very lovely girl down at the Y-Cross Ranch. And I think I'm gonna marry her.

And when the words come out in the open like that so they can't be taken back, with my ma setting on the corner of my bed for a witness, it shocked me even more than her. And scared me too I have to say, because I hadn't had the time or maybe just the courage to dwell

7

on it. But to tell the truth, when I heard those words my-self spoken right out loud, it was as if I was just repeating what had already been signed and sealed and delivered even though I hadn't stopped to wonder if Elizabeth had gotten the same message too. Like as if it was already a settled and complete thing although it hadn't hardly even begun yet. Ma, I says, I met this beautiful girl and I'm gonna marry her.

South Station in Boston early Sunday afternoons, and then back again from Connecticut on the last train north every Sunday night. All through the winter, with me in my old hat and even older sheepskin coat that was per-manently soiled from years of working and feeding ani-mals in it. And seeing that I probably wasn't to be deterred by obstacles of distance or weather, her folks weren't all that happy with me as a prospective suitor for their younger daughter. A student in good standing at one of the world's great learning institutions, I was still by their lights an interloper in a cowboy hat who walked bowlegged in strange boots and talked like he came from a foreign country. Which Wyoming surely was, even though they had had a recent taste of it, compared to the neat and familiar coastline of their Puritan forebears where they had lived all their lives beside the constant ocean. With Boston to the north and east and New York City to the south and west.

Well February roars in and New England or at least that part of it is being battered by what they call an old-fashioned nor'easter. Gale-force winds and nearly two feet of snow that close down just about everything from New York to Boston. Excepting of course the trains, which are still running although on a greatly reduced schedule.

Elizabeth says they're midway through their dinner, each of them at least a little preoccupied with the wild sounds of the storm that if anything seems to have gotten worse, and Mr. Putnam glances down the table at his two daughters and says to Mrs. Putnam, Well the hearth-fire will be a welcome place on a night like this. Carrots please, dear. And Elizabeth says that something makes her turn and look around. And her mother says, It's just the oak limb against the roof, dear. And excusing herself, Elizabeth rises and hurries toward the front entrance where whatever it is seems to knock once again.

And standing there all crusted with snow, she yanks me into the foyer with the wind blowing the snow in too and then shoves the door closed behind me. She doesn't say anything while she wipes the snow from my face and helps me unbutton my coat. For it's at least a three-mile walk from the train station, and I never have gotten into the habit of wearing gloves I guess. And she says, Don't you have any sense at all?

And I say, Ma'm? And then, You mean this little perturbation of wind and weather? Why this is the first time since I left home that it seemed that maybe I really could almost get used to your climate here. And like Pa always said, if horse-sense'd help a jackass be a mule, well nary a man could do any better.

She's standing there trying to keep from shaking her head, with her mouth set and that look in her eyes that is not quite scolding at me just yet. And I say, And besides, I wanted you to marry me. And something in her eyes changes while she tugs on either side of my open coat with her fists against my chest and my back against the door and the snow just beginning to melt onto her arms. And I say, Will you? And she looks into my eyes and just barely tips her head, but nowhere near to actually nodding it. And whispers, Yes.

And I just remember saying, Well then, with the doorknob still in one hand and my hat in the other. And without thinking, or perhaps a bit stunned too along with everything else, I open and close the door behind me lurching down the stairs and back out into the night. And with the wind driving the snow under my open coat and my hat still clutched in my hand as I lumber off into the darkness, I wonder what in God's name had I just done.

I shared rooms with Geoffrey Stuart Coolidge III, and he lends me his old Plymouth, pressing the keys into my hand and telling me that I don't have to take a train to my own damn wedding. This is early in the spring, in April, and there're already buds in the trees. And I remember thinking how back home there's still at least another good month of winter to go. April the tenth.

I leave Cambridge early in the morning with my plan already in hand. For the day before, as I'm studying Coolidge's roadmap, I notice the name a little ways north of New York City. And the symbolism of it or irony or whatever somehow beckons me because I really had no idea where we should do this thing. Elizabeth is watching for me out the window, and as I pull up in front of the house she comes down the walk with a little overnight bag and a coat over her arm. And wearing that same green sweater. Which made me glad when I saw it. Because it helped me forget some of my own nervousness as I recalled her setting up on that corral rail in the last of the twilight when I'd gotten that two-year-old colt gentled and tentatively under control.

As planned, neither of her folks nor her sister were home, and so we were off and headed for western skies. She gets in and hugs me around my neck, tipping my hat off and into the back seat where she'd placed her things. Coolidge had made me wear one of his fine suits, with a necktie and vest, but still permitting me my boots and hat. So at least I'd have something I was used to and familiar with to fall back on in case the realization of what was about to take place started me to doubting either myself or my prospects.

But Elizabeth is just plain excited, with her arm through mine and pressed up beside me as I drive on. With both of my hands gripping the steering-wheel like it was a life-preserver. And watching straight ahead. And hoping to God that we're doing the right thing. Even though I knew all the way back in September when I said it to my ma that we were.

We pass a signpost directing travel toward New York City and go off on a different road. Elizabeth asks me if I know where I'm going and I say, I think so. And she says, Where? And I say, Valhalla. Real serious-like, as if it were the standard and expected destination for anyone bound on such a mission as ours. And she says, Valhalla? And I say, Yes'm, Valhalla New York. For this is probably the single most foolhardy if not to say risky undertaking of my young life. Even considering all the other unpredictable and untamed animals I've ever been associated with. And Valhalla I read somewhere is where they take the dead heroes.

We arrive early in the afternoon and I remember thinking again how mild it was. For I just naturally compared all weather in its season and all fixtures of geography wherever I happened to be to what it would be like if I were back home. Anyway, we drive on to where someone directed us to the town hall. We go into the information office and the woman there sends us over to the revenue office. The clerk doesn't look up from his desk until I say, Excuse me, I'd like to buy a license. And he says, What kind? Dog, fishing or marriage? For he sold them all. And I say, No, marriage.

And then I ask him where I can find a justice of the peace. And he says, There's only one. And he's the presiding judge at the trial. He's the justice of the peace too. And it's this address. He writes something on a slip of paper and hands it to me and says, It's walking distance. And as we leave and proceed toward the main entrance he calls after us, Good luck.

It was one of those big county co-op stores that seem to have a little of everything. Burlap sacks of feed and seed and shelves of hardware and paint. And along one side, utensils and brushes and brooms and shovels. And then more shelves of canned goods amongst bins of nails and tools and probably whatever else you could think of too. But for the most part, the floor had been cleared and then rearranged with parallel rows of folding-chairs. Like in a theatre, with an aisle down the middle. And it looked like the whole town sitting there.

We were holding each other's hand as we stepped inside and everyone turns around to see what had just come through the door. Because apparently the trial was just then right at the height of its emotional intensity. And the judge, a little man with a bald head and a modest mustache and spectacles, looks up at us from the table where he's sitting way down front and says, Whatta you want? Some truckdriver had accidentally killed a woman in the wintertime and he was on trial for causing her death.

We're standing there with our backs against the door like a couple of greenhorns. Young and obviously uninitiated still in the rigors and snares and burdens of it all. And Elizabeth squeezes my hand and presses into me as I look down this blank sea of grim faces all turned about and staring at us. And the little man, who's obviously in charge, leans over his hands and peers over the top of his spectacles and with a trace more of impatience and sternness too he says once again, What do you want?

And I remember thinking how the smell of linseed oil and turpentine is the same everywhere. From that place where I'm standing and where I've never been before, all the way back to home. And maybe a little too loudly when it comes out I answer, We wanna get married!

And once again in almost perfect unison, the faces all turn back around to the front. Their questioning and perhaps disapproving frowns transforming instantly, and however reluctantly, to the unmistakable beginnings of smiles for which they'd had no reason during all the prior proceedings. The judge nods his head one time and says, Okay. And then drawing back from the table and standing he says almost gently, Come down here young people.

We walk down the center aisle through all those strangers, still holding hands. There's sawdust on the floor and what looks like a spill of flour and the definite smell of brine from where two great wooden barrels sit behind the judge's table. And I think I can also smell that dry sharp taste of fresh cheese, for along with everything else I'm also powerful hungry.

And somehow the moment has overtaken both of us so we each know right there and then that we are absolutely and unquestionably where we are meant to be. With all our nameless neighbors in their crowded pews.

And with the judge, who we found out later was really a furniture salesman, waiting for us with his open hands raised and held out before him like a kindly shepherd of the flock ready to send us off in the right direction. And with the blessings of all who are assembled.

For something has transformed the congregation too. One moment, and for three hours previous, at a murder trial. With one of their own accused and aggrieved along with the victim's bereaved family. And with the opening and closing of a door, and the entrance and procession of two very young and somewhat abashed strangers who have appeared inexplicably in their midst and for some reason that is only their own, unexpectedly they have now also become witnesses at a wedding. Thrusting them instantaneously from the dull somber consideration of death to the happy acknowledgment of the unlimited potential of life. From despair unto hopefulness. Like the passing of angels.

Elizabeth presses up against me as we proceed down the aisle, but before we reach him the judge leans forward and says something to someone on either side of the front row. And so the prosecuting attorney stands up beside me as my best man, while the defense attorney rises and stands beside Elizabeth as her full-bearded maid of honor.

The judge instructs each of us in turn. And then digging into my pants-pocket and finding only keys, I experience a moment of real panic that disappears when I find what I'm looking for on my other side. And I give it to him, and then he gives it back to me. And as I turn to Elizabeth, she turns too, and I slide the silver ring onto her finger and continue to hold her hand in mine to steady it, both my hand and hers.

The judge speaks again as we face him. And then turning back to one another we embrace and kiss. And that whole courtroom of strangers, including accused and accuser, still probably more than a little stunned at their unexpected change of perspective, suddenly erupts in a din of applause and cheers as now-wedded and still holding hands we flee back up the aisle and out that same door through which we had first entered.

Angels.

FAMILY

There were summer evenings I remember coming up from the barn after the long day's haying, Spencer says. And seeing Elizabeth through the trees before she could see me. Her apron still about her waist, sitting on the porch steps, and with the warm wind blowing through that beautiful straw-colored hair of hers as she watched at the sky already darkening in the east with that faraway look on her face. As if she could still hear the rising and falling tide that she had grown up with washing up against the bank of the lower meadow.

And I never asked her, for I was shy of her answer

and maybe even a little afraid too of what she might say. Because I always knew in my heart, as the brutal winters wore on, that she suffered us our way of life. And maybe not the way of it so much as its grinding harshness.

That second winter with that filly of hers. I tried to make her understand well before the mare dropped the foal how it was too late in the year in our country for something to be born. Too late for the little one to be able to gain enough strength to make it through the winter. And how when such a thing happened, it was always best for both the mama and the little one to do away with the baby. So the mother could recover herself before the really bad cold set in. And not prolong the life of the little one, for no matter how strong it seemed at birth it would fight a painful battle with winter and lose. For the cold is always that much more powerful than the warm, than the fragile heat of life.

But no, she absolutely refused to hear of it, refused to even consider what I wanted her to understand. Which at the root of it was the very law of the land. Red or one of the other hands happened to be around the barn when the mare went down, shaking and all sweated through. She'd begun to tie-up, which is caused somehow by the muscle enzymes going haywire, and for any number of different reasons. And being pregnant, with her hind end suddenly one big contraction, it had thrown her into labor too although she was still a couple of weeks early.

We finally get ahold of Stony Walls, our vet, just coming in to his dinner, and he comes and goes to work on her. But it seems as if one bad thing follows another. The mare can't really help herself, with her muscles seized up like that, and to top it all off the baby's gonna come breech. Which is when the butt is positioned to deliver first instead of the head.

Stony's up inside her trying to get the foal turned around, but it's just no damn good. And all the while Elizabeth's kneeling close to the mare's head and rubbing up and down her neck whenever she quiets down some, thrashing about and making these godawful groaning sounds and then resting back down again. Stony gets the little one's rear legs started, with the smoke rising off his bare arms, and then Red and I take over for him so's he can have a breather. We sit with our knees against each other pulling steadily on the foal's legs until we can finally see it's a filly for sure, but it seems to hang up on something inside the mare who continues to thrash and grunt against the bed of shavings where she lies.

Elizabeth, I say as I move her hair out of her face, you be right careful for the poor thing's having an awful rough time. And then for one second, the way your mind does, her hands on that distressed animal remind me of my mother's hand on my forehead when I was a little boy and had to stay home from school. And then that image jumps all the way into the future and turns back into Elizabeth's hand again but this time on the forehead of one of our own children who as far as I know hadn't even gotten started yet.

Stony gets between Red and me once again, nudging us off to either side, and reaches back inside the mare until he gets the foal's one foreleg that was bent and holding it back freed up the way it needs to be. He continues to pull against its hind legs until suddenly the baby rushes out of her, knocking Stony on his back and lying on top of him. He finally straightens up with the baby clasped in his arms and just sits there like that.

You alright? I ask him. And he tells me he wants whatever blood that's left in the placenta to get into the foal before he cuts it loose from the mama. The mare lies back with her head stretched out and Stony ties off the cord and then carries the foal into the next stall. Elizabeth's brought him a couple of blankets and he kneels in the corner with the baby beneath them and his arms around it like before, with its head over his shoulder. And I can still see its lovely little face with its big eyes blinking with wonder in the gloom of the barn as if it were thinking to itself, So this is life. So this is what the fuss is all about.

Elizabeth stays with the baby, and Stony draws off the mare's first milk and then tube-feeds it into the foal through its nostril to be sure she gets all of it into her stomach. It's past nine o'clock and I send Red home for he's got a full day in the morning, and of course I do too. But as it turns out, the night has just begun.

When an animal ties-up like that, its kidneys will eventually shut down which will lead to its death. So our only chance of keeping the mare alive is to keep running fluids into her until she's urinating normally, which should indicate that her kidneys are still OK. But then it's still a damn crapshoot, because if there's been too much muscle damage she wouldn't be any good for herself anyway.

Stony had come prepared for the long haul when we'd described to him over the phone what was happening. And so he'd brought with him several cases of those electrolyte fluid-bags along with a week's supply of milk-replacement for the baby. And he gets himself all set up like he knows that tomorrow's a hell of a long ways off but he still intends to be there with the mare alongside him and that they'll both see the morning together.

He sews a catheter into her jugular vein and then

hangs the first of the clear plastic bags from a hook he's screwed into an overhead beam. Then he attaches a long transparent tube that goes from the bottom of the bag into the portal at the mare's neck. And I watch with him for a few minutes as the liquid begins to drip and fall.

Elizabeth's mixed up a batch of that milk-replacement, and she's got a baby-bottle of it with a rubber nipple, and she's setting in the next stall talking to the foal and rubbing its forehead and trying to get it interested in what she's got to offer. I kneel down with her and tell her that I'll get the baby started, and could she get Stony some dinner, which reminds me that we hadn't had our own yet either. And she goes off.

Well the baby keeps nosing around the bottle in my hand with that wonderful soft skin of the newborn, and I'm setting up against her as Elizabeth had been and probably mumbling some of that same foolishness in the foal's ear as I watch her eyes wide and new. And her eyelashes when she blinks somehow make me smile. She finally gets it in her mind to try what's behind the nipple and begins drawing at it, with those lovely eyes of hers going back and forth and every now and again looking right at me.

Looks to me like she's found her a daddy, Stony says. And I look up to see him standing against the opening to the stall with his arms crossed on his chest and a big

smile on that mug of his. The mare's quiet, he says. We'll keep the fluids to her as long as it takes. Will she eat anything? I ask him. And he says, Oh she'll nibble at some grain every now and again but she's not real interested. The baby takes another bottle of the milk substitute and then just puts its chin down on its knee and closes its eyes and goes to sleep. And I move away and close the stall door real quiet-like so's it'll take its rest.

We all eat in the runway between the stalls with Stony periodically checking on the mare. He's got three of those fluid-bags strung together and hanging there so it gives us time to eat our dinner. But while we're still at it, there's a thrashing from the baby's stall and we look in at her just beginning to get her legs. She gets her hind legs under her and nearly locked and pauses like that, quivering, but when she goes to rise up off her elbows she rocks back and falls over.

Stony's gone back to the mare and Elizabeth goes in to the foal. She'll do'er, I say, standing back and watching. For it's always been a miracle to me, the birth, and then seeing them make themselves stand upright and soon after bouncing and jumping around like they'd been practicing their locomotion for months instead of just hours.

Elizabeth crouches in the corner beside the little thing as it somehow forces itself back into the same position. Pushing up its hind legs all aquiver, and with its lit-

tle tail sucked right flat against its butt. Elizabeth slides her open hands under its belly, not hardly touching it, and as it pushes up off its front and starts over again she supports underneath it so that all four legs are straight and locked. It hesitates for just a moment, still trembling with its new little muscles that only an hour or so ago had been what it only needed to paddle with in the warm safe waters of the womb. And then it extends one foreleg for its first step, but before getting it accomplished it pitches forward and dives woefully back onto its face.

Don't take very much to learn to fall, Stony says quietly beside me. But the getting back up again, I say, the will to get back up. Aye, Stony says, for each and every one of us I reckon. And inside myself I say, Amen. And then again, A-men.

We get Stony all fixed up with a pillow and that ancient great-grandma's quilt that must weigh fourteen or fifteen pounds at least. Elizabeth feeds her filly again which had been sleeping on its side weary from the hard journey it'd traveled that evening. All the way from that far inland sea which is all it'd ever known before being cast up on a rough and fearful shore. And then more wondrous than frightening amid the quiet hours of myriad discovery, it had found itself not seacreature at all but something apparently unsuited to its new environment.

A fragile tottering stick-legged thing, having known

its first hunger and then perhaps its first independent dream too of unimagined places where its legs once they worked more harmoniously might take it. For it had finally managed its first few precarious steps, and known warmth again after its startling discovery of the cold, and recovered the darkness too after its incomprehensible discovery of the light. And there appeared to be many mothers for its choosing. None that slept beside it just then but many kindly mothers nonetheless.

Stony tells Elizabeth that he'll feed the baby through the night as long as he's right there, for she'll no longer have such a luxury after he leaves. But, No, she says, she reckons where she'll be in that baby's stall every two hours for the next three days. And then she'll proceed from there onward until the poor little thing is ready for weaning. And I can see right then and there that this whole event is about to provide an actual treasure of learning for someone, and as I walk back up to the house by myself I figure that I'm probably the one that's about to be reeducated. For Elizabeth seems to know just precisely where this whole affair is headed. And I'll be damned if she isn't up and down all night long those first few days.

And when the filly can finally go for four whole hours between feedings, it almost seems like a vacation, at least to me and our alarm-clock. Like when you get a spate of twenty- or thirty-below-zero weather, and it sets in real good and firm sometime after the new year. Why, a rise up to say five-below-zero is near to almost being downright tropical. And a day that actually makes it all the way back to zero, so you're neither on the plus or the minus, why that's practically shirtsleeve weather. Making you wonder as you leave the house if you really do need your coat or not. And although you've still got nearly five months to go, you know that spring is absolutely inevitable. And hellfire, why a man's hopefulness can just about soar on rosy new wings unfettered.

I've already finished shaving and I'm nearly dressed when the alarm goes off for the six o'clock feeding. I tell Elizabeth that I'll take care of that one, and I'll see her by suppertime. I guess she'd fixed Stony some food at the four o'clock, and as I enter the barn all is quiet. I creep past the baby's stall and see that she's asleep with her legs stretched out straight as if she were dreaming of standing squarely upright. And then I look in at the mare and Stony and, I'll be, I whisper to myself.

The lights over each of the stalls are off but the ones that are spaced further apart over the runway are still on. The last one is opposite the mare's stall so that the baby lies in near darkness, while a dim half-light spreads over most of Stony and the mama.

He's got the fluid dripping at a slower rate and of the three bags that hang there she's almost finished with the second one. A couple of empty plates are stacked on top of each other and pushed off to one side with a fork laid across them. And Stony is setting in the bedded shavings with his back leaning away from the wooden partition and his legs out before him. And with the mare's face lying across his lap.

He's still got the quilt wrapped about his shoulders but it's nearly fallen off one side of him. His left arm is turned away from the horse, with the fingers of that hand almost touching a saucer that holds an empty teacup. As if he had just had time to set it down before sleep had finally overtaken him, in midstride so to speak. His other arm lies across the mare's neck, and his face rests on her head. And they're both sound asleep.

All God's creatures, I think as I stand there watching them. And the beauty of it, of the oneness of all life, just about freezes me so that I am almost afraid that if I blink I might disturb them. All God's creatures.

TOMATOES

Behind the house and out the kitchen window with the mountains shimmering violet and white in the distance, all the summer's bedlinen ballooned and flapped in the wind. Like the furling snapping sails of an imaginary old schooner that had somehow run aground in the tall green pasture before making it back to the level swaying ocean somewhere beyond. That none of the three boys had ever seen.

Luke and Whitney raced each other up the stairs but Whitney got there first, grabbing the compass that Lonny, their older brother, had given them and shown them how to use. And that they both tried to watch at the same time as they came bumping back down. Until Whitney had to catch at the banister, so that Luke could snatch it away. But then Whitney grabbed it right back even before the little red needle had ceased turning. There was a tin with pie left in it on the kitchen counter that Whitney said was west of the stairs, but when Luke plucked the compass back out of his hands he corrected the heading as actually being west-northwest.

They took the pie tin to the table and stood there with each of the two pieces dripping through their fingers and crushed against their faces. Their father, Spencer, was off with the haying and Lonny was with him. They didn't know where their mother, Elizabeth, was for the pickup was gone too. But surely not all the way into Lewiston because this was Saturday and she always went to town on Monday.

The sunlight glared through the window and over the floor and up the table where they stood with their mouths full, chewing madly to see who could finish first with bright red cherry-fruit all over them like a paint. They both went to the sink at the same time. Luke dragged the stepstool up so they could stand and thrust their hands under the rushing water that bounded off both of them like they were puppies in a bath.

The bedsheets through the window were like gleaming bright banners sailing away from the lines that anchored them until the wind fell, and then they looked like big whitewashed walls lacking ornament or artifice. The mountains seemed to ripple in the sun almost purple and with a silver band of old snow that never melted completely outlining each peak and saddle as if they were the seldom exposed ramparts of the fortress of the world that you could only see glimpses of for a month or two in the middle of summer before the snows returned to cover them up all over again. And just then the mountains seemed to ride on top of the sheets, which were flapping again like massive white wings. And on the other side of the tomatoes.

Arranged in neat rows on the sash of the lower half of the window and crowded up against each other on the sill and the ledge above the sink where the bar of soap and the bottle of detergent and the sponge had all been moved aside so that as many tomatoes as could fit in that parallelogram of almost blinding brightness could bask and sun in safety. Already red and just about ripe and obviously set there to ripen even further, that Elizabeth must have brought back from the greenhouse in East Lewiston because there wasn't ever enough time where they lived to grow tomatoes down on the ground. What with how late spring arrived and then only that brief respite from the cold that they called summer squeezed in between the end of June and the end of August. And with that prescient suspicion of October already coloring the wind somehow like a precursor sometimes just after dusk.

And so there just wasn't enough time. Whether in the high valley that protected the town of Lewiston nearly eighteen miles away or higher still amongst the vast ranchlands carved out of the government territory long ago that couldn't be called a settlement with any manner of confederation except that one fortunate tributary ran through most of it. And too, with one of the original old homesteader's cabins centrally situated where Doris Moore still lived, widowed and with her children long grown and gone, as postmaster of what had always been called as long as anyone could remember, Lime Creek.

And even called Lime Creek in each of their tongues by the Shoshone and the Cheyenne and the Crow and the Sioux who at one time or another had also used that land long before the Whiteman. And with all the other creatures that of course had always been there even before them, but that needed no names. Neither for themselves nor for that harsh and beautiful place on the earth that was their home too. Lime Creek.

And so there just wasn't enough time to grow things like tomatoes. And if you were ever tempted to try when the ground got warm and it stayed warm at night which was above freezing, blooming an almost childish optimism that maybe even persisted until the first frost which was sometimes as early as the middle of September with the leaves in the high country already beginning to change in secret pockets until you could almost see it in the very quality of the light thickening somehow as the age of the year slowly declined, then you'd no longer be able to convince yourself that perhaps this time you might succeed. And having known it right from the start. And so all the bounty of your careful ministrations just those early rock-hard green tomatoes the size and consistency of golfballs that only needed the warm and enough time, which they could never get. At least not in that country.

Both little boys reached together to close the faucet, and then used opposite ends of the same dishtowel to more or less dry their hands. The mountains of course had always been there, but that sudden new perspective with all those bright red tomatoes and all of a perfect size and shape staring them right in the face—and just beyond, of those gleaming white sheets that for the moment hung limp again like empty flat canvases almost begging to be used—transfixed both of them and at the same time moved their instincts down the same identical path.

Whitney puts his thumb on the biggest one just to see what it feels like, with Luke leaning over his shoulder. And then to their amazement Whitney's thumbnail just disappears. They both look at each other with less than an instant of consternation that almost simultaneously bursts into peals of such rollicking laughter that they nearly fall off their stance. And then without another thought or even another word and imbued with that perfect knowledge of what must be done, Luke is standing down and Whitney is carefully piling each of the tomatoes in Luke's arms which are cradled against his chest. Perhaps about a quarter-bushel of ripe tomatoes that reaches all the way up past his chin.

Then Whitney climbs down and gingerly takes half of his brother's burden in his own arms and against his own chest and so against his own little heart too. And slowly and more carefully than anything they can ever remember doing, they shuffle through the kitchen and the pantry until the screen-door pushes open against Luke's shoulder and they are once again outside. The ground falls away as they go around the back of the house, and with the kitchen window now high above them they suddenly stand before those great bright unsullied surfaces that call to them not so much with their emptiness as with all the wondrous possibilities for filling it.

They both crouch down resting on their knees and then leaning onto their elbows like supplicants until the tomatoes roll off them and onto the ground at last, where they form them into two even and equal rows. All summer long Lonny had been throwing a hardball at a wooden crate that had been nailed to the outside of the barn, and even though its sides were all splintered and shattered away, its outline was still fixed there for a target. And now Luke and Whitney had targets of their own. Big and snow-white and so inviting that even if they couldn't throw as good as Lonny, they still couldn't miss.

They alternated back and forth and from one to the other. Luke first, the shocking red blossom of his tomato exploding against the sheet dead-center, and a moment later Whitney's right beside it. Understanding as they took aim that they must also take their time and concentrate on every pitch so as to fully take advantage of such a gifted opportunity. And so as the spectre of each imaginary batter flailed away unsuccessfully, rosy starlike murals began to emerge from their works-in-progress, crowning the meadow and celebrating the mountains and obviously birthing a virtuosity in both of them that hitherto hadn't been foreseen. But that never was appreciated either.

They were up in the hayloft with the compass again when Spencer comes into the barn and says, You boys get on down here. Not loud but hard enough so they know it isn't about supper. They climb down the ladder and when they turn at the bottom, Spencer's standing in the door with those sheets that they'd already forgotten about hanging over his shoulder. He also has suspended from one hand that big galvanized tub that Elizabeth gives Lemon his bath in, and a loop of harness-rein still neatly coiled in the other as if he had just gotten it down from in the tackroom. His head keeps shaking slowly from side to side. Boys, he says again. Lonny isn't with him. Get that sawhorse.

Which they do, one on either end. And which is how they position themselves too, draped over at the waist with their heads and arms hanging over one side and their legs over the other. A second sawhorse, with a bull's skull attached to one end that Lonny practiced his roping on, stares at them with its great hollow eyesockets. Free of judgment of course, but still watching them as if to divine by the severity of the punishment the magnitude of their crime.

Each time the harness-strap falls, cracking like a whip beside their inside hips, they flinched up so bad that they nearly sprang off the hard two-by-four cross-bar from which they hung like little soiled upside-down birds. But the strap always miraculously missed them, each sharp report detonating beside one little boy and then the other and then back and forth again. And then again. Until finally after the fourth go-round Spencer says, Alright. Get up. And at the same time hearing Elizabeth in his mind just as clear as if she were standing next to him saying, Well I don't guess that poor sawhorse is gonna cause any more trouble. After that.

They slide backward until their feet touch down and then stand there watching at their sneakers as if fascinated by the tomato stains that have turned their shoes pink as well as by the constellations of little seeds that are stuck to all the laces. You boys carry this tub, Spencer says. They don't ask where. And get that grain-bucket too. Give it here. He drops something hard in it, and while they carry the tub between them, Spencer holds the pail with the block of soap. And under his other arm, the old washboard that Elizabeth keeps behind the washing-machine. And with both of the soiled sheets still hanging over his shoulder.

By the time they get to the creek it's dark on the ground through the trees. They have to keep stopping to rest the tub down as they go, and once or twice they try to drag it along the ground but that just makes it even harder because the bottom keeps catching in the dirt. Heavy, ain't it? Spencer says. Maybe you boys shoulda thoughta that before making such a mess. And them to-maters, you can give your ma your Christmas money for them tomaters. Least if you're rich enough, which I'm guessing you're probably not. I just don't know, he says shaking his head.

They try to drag the tub once again and then Whit-ney picks up his end and Luke his. It's dark and fixing to cool off even colder because when the sun goes down the temperature falls nearly thirty degrees no matter what time of year it is. Finally they can hear the water on the other side of the trees. Spencer drops the sheets on the ground in a pile and then the bucket so the brick of soap bangs against its side. And then the washboard.

Now that soap doesn't ever get near that water, he says, because no fish anywhere has to get sick too because of you boys. Understand? They both look up and whis-per, Sir. And Spencer has to quickly turn his head to pre-tend to cough behind his hand so they can't see his face, which has to smile when he looks at them whatever they've done. Like two little soldiers in short-sleeve jer-seys with filthy faces and miniature jeans and crushed fruit all over their sneakers. As if that was that day's image of love. Two little soldiers of love, one with black hair and the other sandy-colored and sticking up every which way like roostertails, with streaked faces and eyes afraid to look up at him as he coughs and turns away again to hide his open smile and also to get his voice back to where it still sounded the way it should.

Understand? he says again. You keep that soap away from that crick. Sir, they say again. You can take turns, he says, filling up this tub. No, you better go together because a bucket that's filled up is heavy enough for two. You get this tub filled up and get them two godawful sheets as clean as you found them. You hear me? They look up from their shoes again, this time just nodding their heads. Now get, he says and turns away.

They place the soap on the jumbled mass of bed-sheets and then take up the bucket with each of one of their little hands clasped together on the handle, bumping and clanking through the shore trees and down to where the bank juts out and forms a protected shoal where they'd always previously only gone to swim. There's a huge cottonwood tree overhead, the biggest one that anyone around there had ever seen. It was actually two trunks that had grown together and become one, and there was a fire-circle of big stones at its base.

Lonny had once read them the story about the old couple long ago who, having been the only hospitable humans that the gods disguised as vagabonds had encountered when they came down to earth, were granted any wish that they desired. And without hesitation, they both replied that their only fear was that one of them would die and leave the other one alone. And so if the gods could arrange it, all they really wanted was to depart from this life together. Zeus and his sidekick Mercury bowed and went on their way. And behind them, where the old folks' hut had stood, two great trees grew up as one with their trunks intertwined and their branches holding each other for all time. And to Luke and Whitney and probably to Lonny too, their cottonwood was that tree.

But just then Whitney and Luke aren't thinking about stories or even about trees, and when Spencer hears them clashing the bucket again against the ground he's already built up a little peak of orange and yellow flames to greet them. Half a bucket isn't gonna be so heavy, he says. And we got all night now, don't we boys?

They don't look up as they lug the bucket with contorted grimaces on both of their faces. And with all four of their hands grasping the handle they almost walk over one another with each awkward step that also casts a tongue of glinting water up their legs. And so by the time they reach the tub the pail's only about a third-full. And you tend this fire too, Spencer says, before it gets too dark and cold. Hear?

I'm gonna get me some supper. And boys, he says, raising his voice so they pause and turn with the uneven light playing on their faces and making menacing shapes of all the trees, don't even think of bringing those sheets home until they look as clean as you found them. He watches their blank downturned expressions and then turns behind his hand again, releasing them to clatter back down to the water. Mind the fire now, he yells, and turns to go.

It takes them a long time to get the tub filled and to keep the fire going too. And while they're still gathering brush and anything else that'll burn, Lemon rushes up to them with little points of the pitiful flame reflected in his eyes and starts licking Whitney's arm that must still have some of that cherry flavor from the pie adhered above his elbow. Whitney grunts and pushes Lemon away, and still wagging his tail like one of those piano metronomes Lemon runs over to Luke who's on his hands and knees in search of whatever fuel he can find, and turns him too by licking the side of his face. Just as Spencer's legs come up in the dark and then kneel down behind the rosy glow that's nearly expired.

He must have brought something combustible with

him because when both little boys look up again he's built a pyramid of kindling and branches that when he blows on it makes the fire jump up brighter and more welcoming than anything they can ever remember. Or at least right then anyway. Lemon runs back and forth between them with the fire dancing in his eyes and his tail going a mile a minute, and then when Spencer pats at the ground beside him Lemon sits and kind of collapses in stages against Spencer's leg.

Well that tub's full enough I reckon, Spencer says, but I still don't see anything getting washed in it. He's sitting against the tree with his legs spread out before him while he undoes the top of a brown paper bag. Your ma says them boys need some supper so they can get their work done. And I say I don't know as they deserve any supper. And she says to give'em this to keep their strength up. And to give'em their sweatshirts too.

Both boys come and sit in the dirt on either side of their father's legs with their backs to the bright cheery flames as they pull over their heads the long-sleeve shirts that he hands them. Then they shyly accept the sandwiches that he offers, almost with a deference that's clearly in obverse ratio to the ferocity with which they fall to eating. Bacon and lettuce, Spencer says. Your ma apologizes for the missing tomaters to make'em taste right. Which is lost on them anyway as they chew mightily to clear their full cheeks, like chipmunks that can't hardly swallow fast enough. Spencer makes himself cough again so he can turn his head all the way around this time and silently laugh outright.

Because maybe it's just them durn sneakers, he thinks. But no, when he can watch them again of course it's their faces, with dirt and cherry and doglick and black and fair thatches of hair stuck up everywhere. And yet still contentedly just chewing away, having already forgotten apparently the actual reason that they're there in the first place. Until Spencer's voice says, with his face out of the firelight, When're them bedsheets gonna get done, boys? Cause eventually I need to get me some sleep. You boys, he says again and shakes his head. I gotta full day's haying in the morning and here I am having a picnic in the middle of the night with two actual outlaws. And he thinks, and with their wanted-posters on every laundry-room wall too.

And so finally there's nothing else for them but their waiting penance. Soaking wet with the washboard leaned against the inside of the tub and that great unworkable mass of bedlinen that's more like a dull mute creature sucking on their arms and flopping against their chests and slapping at their faces. Almost like that tarbaby Lonny had read to them about, and how it says Biff every time it catches one arm and then the other and one leg and then the other until Brer Rabbit says to Brer Fox, You can do anything you want except please please don't throw me in that brierpatch. Which was really the one place Brer Rabbit could go so he could finally escape.

Because it seemed like that thing that they had fed and watered and so given life to was somehow gaining in strength at the same time that theirs was diminishing, for every time they tried to move it around and shove parts of it up against the ridges of the washboard that also hurt their hands, it grabbed at them and drew them closer and closer into the cold sudsy water where it lived. And while Lemon still circled excitedly from Whitney to Luke and then back again, and while the little fire began to die down once more, and while they wrestled with the thing as if locked in mortal combat on their knees and with their little bodies half-sunk over the side of the tub as if knowing full well that if they finally succumbed they might well be lost. And perhaps even swallowed whole. Like those flowers that closed around a fly and then just ate it.

When they stopped once to rest they could hear Spencer's breathing, who hadn't said anything for a long time like he was asleep. Then one of his boots kind of

44

kicks out like it had suddenly come awake and he says, Boys, I ain't as strong as you little boys anymore cause I need to get up to my bed. So if you boys're staying, you tend that fire. Hear? His legs stand up so they can't see past his knees for the dying of the firelight. But if you're done, he says, and they watch up at him with a sudden and unanticipated hopefulness. Well, bring them cleaned sheets. You can come back for everything else in the morning. And turn that tub over. I don't want no critter getting a bellyache of soapy water either.

They struggle to lift up the mass of bedlinen that by then weighs almost as much as they do themselves, but it just lies there on the bottom of the tub. Finally Spencer bends over and grabs up one of the sheets and then the other. Set that washboard down, he says. They just manage to get it out of the water before it falls from their wrinkled little hands that they can't hardly feel anymore, clattering off the edge of the tub and coming to rest in the red clayey dirt at Spencer's feet.

That'll do, he says, with the big dripping wad in both hands that he lays down on the board so the sides of it flop over in the dirt too. Both little boys kneel behind the tub trying to push up under it until Spencer bends over again and lifts up so the sudsy water and then the block of soap cascade out and splash against the ground.

Spencer lifts it all the way up on its edge with the little boys walking under it with their hands upraised as if they were pushing against it too, until it balances for an instant on its fulcrum and then topples over covering where the incongruity of the soap bubbles melt against the earth.

Spencer raises each of the sheets one at a time and then folds and turns them like a twist of rope with more of the water raining on the ground. Then he drapes one of them over Luke's shoulders like a lady's stole that hangs down either side of his little chest so his arms must rest against it. Whitney hangs back a step as if he were still contemplating the overturned tub, but comes back around when the filthy wet garment is draped over his shoulders too.

Now get on, Spencer says, and don't wake up your ma. I'll mind the fire. He kneels down with the tentative flame still aglow on his face and watches them as they stiffly move away. Lemon paces between them, darting ahead and trotting back and then running ahead of them once again, like the horses pulling against their reins in the direction of the barn no matter how far away it is. Or like those pilgrims, bowing toward their holyland when they prayed, which in most cases was somewhere on the other side of the world.

The ends of each of the sheets drag in the dirt and catch on sage and scrub as both little boys go, receding lopsided ghost shapes that dimly reflect the light from the stars and the peel of the new moon hanging somewhere between the barn and the distant wall of the invisible mountains. And then Spencer can no longer see them nor hear them either. But all the way across the meadow and raised up in that same darkness, they are bound toward that one constant light behind that one upstairs window that still persists in that vast and sightless night, like a golden yellow fragile hopeful thing to show them the way. And back to where they started from.

Spencer builds up the fire for himself and watches into it sitting with his back against the tree until his eyes close listening to the slow low creek of the end of summer clucking across its eternal bed of smooth and priceless stones. Listening. Eventually he senses that the dying firelight no longer interrupts the darkness and he stirs with his arms still folded on his chest. The fire has become just two glowing orange coils of ash. He pushes himself up groaning to himself and then crushes what's left of it and scatters it with his boot. When he turns he sees that the moon has moved closer to the barn, while the yellow light in the upstairs window farther on still reassures him as if it somehow anchored the close even arc of his life, along with those other beloved lives that slept behind it waiting for him.

He always limped some the first few steps when he stood up until he walked through it and through the stiffness. And to him his limp was Parker and somehow Parker's abiding presence. His best friend in the War and truly his brother-in-arms. And so Spencer was glad that it was there because he never wanted to forget him. And of course he never would. Because that was the first lesson of war. Not the horror, which is its other name. But love. Because knowing you're about to die, and that the person beside you is about to die too, all of what makes you who you are in an instant of fear so intense that it stops your breath and nearly stops your heart too, disappears. And all that is left is love. Unquantifiable love for the other man who for one more moment is still there beside you. Only love.

And so Spencer's limp always reminded him of Parker, and especially of Parker's eyes, which he also had never been able to forget. Not one day since that day. And since that moment when he watched them change, with Parker's head lying in his lap. And then in place of Parker's eyes frightened and questioning were the eyes of a statue that no longer could see him and turning to stone.

So that was Spencer's lameness when he first stood up and not the arthritis nor the jag of the ill-healed bone. It was Parker and the machine-gun fire that hadn't let up all day since pinning them down, and Spencer's own life slowly ebbing away beneath the imperfect tourniquet made of his torn sleeve that he had bound about the top of his right leg. Until he suddenly realizes that the round olive-drab boulder in the grass that somehow he hadn't noticed before was actually the top of a helmet. Was actually Parker inching towards him on his belly to try to help him. Until something that neither of them ever saw seems to just barely lift Parker and at the same time knock him backwards. And he doesn't move again.

And so finally dragging Parker to lie with his head on him while he sits back against the blasted tree trunk that still shielded him from the ceaseless wind of death that was all around them. That was Parker and the mortal scar torn down the length of the outside of Spencer's thigh that resembled a broad shiny sword of flesh with little shiny lace-holes like buttons all up and down either side of it.

And then, reminded of his scar, he sees himself and his three boys upstairs in the bathroom after that tremendous water-fight that Lonny had started with the can of shavefoam that Spencer had set out on the sink.

Lying in the empty tub and playing the cool water over him with the rubber hose he'd attached to the tub spigot in the days before he'd put in the shower. And before he'd been attacked, with shaving-cream and water all over the black and white floor, and Elizabeth standing for a moment in the door with her hands all white with flour, and them letting her have it too so she jumps back into the hall and maybe even floats back downstairs.

And then finally spent, they declare a truce so they can all dry themselves. And Whitney touches the broad shiny scar that almost covers the outside of Spencer's upper leg and says, What's that? with his finger still resting there. And Spencer says, while rubbing his own head with his towel, That's where your pa got hurt a long time ago. Then he lets the towel down at his side and sits on the curved edge of the tub. Somebody with a gun, Spencer says. And Lonny says, In the War, right Pa? And Spencer says, That's right son, in the War. And Luke asks, How come? And by then each of the boys is also dry and Whitney and Luke sit on the edge of the tub to Spencer's right while Lonny sits on his other side. And Spencer's outspread arms like wings enfold them all.

Because in the War, Spencer says, people go to hurt each other. With guns. And Luke says once again, How come? And Spencer looks at the two little boys and says almost in a whisper, I don't know boys. I don't really know if anyone knows. And Whitney says, Then why do they do it? And Spencer shakes his head as he watches the open window filled with green leaves that make a soft clattering sound when the warm wind blows, and tells them how people shoot the guns at each other to try to hurt each other. And that a bullet from one of the guns had gone into his leg and broken the bone. And Whitney asks, Did you do it too, Pa? And Spencer says, What? And Whitney says, Shoot the guns at the people? And Spencer whispers, Yes. And Luke says, How come? And Spencer whispers, I don't know. And then as if he were really just talking to himself, I don't know if I'll ever know.

And so that was Spencer's limp that disappeared altogether after his first five or six steps. And if you hadn't been looking for it, expecting it when he stood up, you wouldn't have even known it was there. Unless he was angry or in a hurry or both, and then it might come back again until something inside him would just bear down somehow and make it go away. Until the next time.

He could feel the night dew collecting on his boots as he followed the stubble where the first swath of hay had been mown. Above him infinitely familiar and far was Orion's belt of stars with its lesser sword, and brightest of all Sirius the home of the gods and where all wisdom was supposed to have come from. The Hunter and his Dog forever tracking Taurus across the northern summer sky. Then he watched up at the yellow bedroom window once more with his steps even and sure so that whatever hurt there may have been in the bone, or perhaps in the heart, was hidden inside him again and no longer made manifest to the night.

He turns the wick down in the ancient lantern on the nighttable beside the bed. Elizabeth is sound asleep and turned so she faces the open window with its delicate veil of a curtain, and with the shallow hump of her shoulder risen up beneath the quilt. Then he stands in the dark hall on the other side of Lonny's open door listening to his first-born son's breathing, and somehow satisfied he proceeds toward that same bathroom where a narrow strip of light now outlines the bottom of its door. He stands and listens once again but hears nothing. Then the slow steady drip of a faucet as if it were nearly closed but not quite. He silently turns the knob and enters.

A second door opposite him opens into the little boys' room, and their light is on too. A haphazard trail of empty sneakers and formless garments flung every which way as if their erstwhile occupants hadn't had time enough to discard them before taking their leave runs from the sink across the tiled floor and through the other door where two little naked bodies are cast up on what could be if he narrows his eyes marooned pieces of some recent and obvious shipwreck.

Luke is turned upside-down clinging acrobatically to the foot of his bed so he seems to balance at just such an angle as to hang above the floor however precariously. His pillow hides the back of his head and his eyes are closed and his mouth open, but his breath makes no sound. His blankets are twisted up in his feet so one leg and buttock and one shoulder and arm are left uncovered.

Whitney sprawls on his back clutching his blankets to his chest but his legs hang over the side with one foot resting on Lemon's shoulder, who sleeps beneath him on the floor. Whitney's eyes are closed too and as he breathes behind his pressed lips he makes a faint buzzing sound as if a honeybee were caught inside him trying to find a way out.

Spencer closes the overhead light in the boys' room so a flat pale wedge from the bathroom still shines across the floor. He places his hands under Luke and lifts him into the center of his bed, rearranging his covers and pillow so his dirty face and hands are all that are left exposed. And of course still smelling of little boys in his hair all mixed up with sage and raw soap and cherry and dog. When he lifts Whitney, he rolls over so Spencer has to lift him again to get his blankets out from under him. Whitney sighs and his buzzing grows still when he lies his head back on his pillow smelling exactly like Luke, an amalgam of sweat and claydirt and soap and sugarcherry, and his face and arms and hands are just as dirty.

Lemon makes a sound when he yawns that's like opening a door with hinges that haven't been oiled in a long time, and as Spencer finishes tending to Whitney the dog's tail beats happily against the floor. When Spencer finally turns from the bed he bends down and kneads Lemon's muscular shoulders and neck so he lies his chin on Spencer's foot until Spencer moves away, passing silently back through the bathroom and into the hall.

When he returns, the dog has gone back to sleep too and both boys are in exactly the same positions as he had left them. He places a piece of notepaper on top of their clothes-bureau, which still has half its drawers open with garments and socks spilling over and hanging down. And a five-dollar bill that almost covers the one word that he's printed on the paper in pencil. Tomatoes. Then he retrieves one of the little sneakers and places it on top of the money and the piece of paper so the soft breeze in the window curling the filmy curtains won't blow them away. Tomatoes.

Inextricably joined from then on, like the rewiring of dissimilar synapses that once touched together become fused so in the fabric of memory. Immutable, irrepressible and inviolable to everything except death. Tomatoes. Forever after inspiring images that have little to do with the nourishment of the flesh. But like everything else having everything to do with the feeding of the soul.

Tomatoes.

SLEEP

The barn was closed off to us the whole day of Christmas Eve, Luke says. Because Spencer, our father, would be working there no matter how cold it was. And I remember how small we were, Whitney and me, wrestling and tumbling over each other. And how Lonny, our older brother, was always the leader. And so we always wanted to do what Lonny was doing. And too, how Lonny seemed to have this patient kindness for us, the almost-grown shepherd to his tiny flock of half-wild little boys.

And at that same time my memory of Elizabeth, our mother, is always of her cooking all day. And the smells of it building and carrying us in a fever of expectation until it would reach a kind of fragrant crescendo that by the time we would finally sit down to Christmas dinner would have nearly exhausted all our senses. Her having to stop in the midst of her chores to see that we were bundled up enough against the cold and then ushering us toward the door with Lonny taking us each by the hand. You boys can walk up towards Doris's to see those Christmas lights, she says, but I want you home again before it gets dark please.

We wanna ride Blue, Whitney says. The biggest animal that Whitney and I were allowed to be around. A great big sixteen-and-a-half-hand blue roan gelding as gentle as a long-legged old grandfather who had to be wary of where he placed his feet so that he would do nothing to jeopardize that unhurried gait of his, tired and knobbly but still eventually getting him where he figured he needed to go. And so solicitously careful when we were about him that in later years I often wondered if he had gained an instinct for us as being small two-legged creatures somehow akin to the phantom sons and grandsons never yet birthed into being but who still may have lived in his imagination behind that singular and imperturbable regard of his that was always on his greying face, bespeaking a boundless kind-eyed forbearance that somehow in the ancient way of the beast loved the young, the foals and the puppies and the little boys too.

And Elizabeth says, Not today boys. You mind that barn, Lonny, and be back before it's dark. And Lonny says, Yes'm. And then we're bumping and shoving each other along the frozen road that's become the bottom of a topless tunnel between story-high snowbanks, eventually crossing both snowed-over cattleguards and then the culvert where the buried creek runs along that side of the ranch.

And then it would be dark and we'd finally leave the house to go down to the barn, and the sky behind the high country would just barely yet hold the very last of the light so that if you didn't think to watch for it you'd miss it, the day's end. There'd be four or five pickup trucks parked below the barn, and my remembrance is always of a crystal-clear moonless night with the temperature already below zero and the snow crunching so loud under our boots that you could even hear the steps of the other people and their kids walking up from where they'd left their vehicles.

And the stars by then, the stars seemed so big in the sky that you'd think you could almost hear them too like the burning of distant torches if you were to stop and really listen. There was this one huge one in the east in the winter that shone with different colors, and it stayed there all through the cold. Whitney and I assumed it to be the same star that all the stories talked about, but Lonny told us sometime later that it was in the constellation of the Dog. And we liked knowing that because our lives down here on the ground were so intertwined with animals that it only seemed natural for the stars to have a similar frame of reference too.

You could hear Toebowman's guitar from inside the barn when you were still a little ways off, Bradley Bowman's uncle Tobin who everyone called Toebowman as if his two names first and last were really one name put together. The sound of the guitar in the delicate clarity of the newborn night made everybody quiet as we approached, the loveliness of it so achingly simple and pure from out of the whelming darkness like an earth-bred accompaniment to a universe cut from glass. With the crunching snow and that simple human refrain on this side of the cold, and the stars so familiar and yet so distant on the other side.

Whitney and I and Lonny would all have fallen into that hush as we walked, and Elizabeth would squeeze my hand in my mitten without saying anything. And I could see her face in my mind without having to look up at her. We'd all be still as we entered the barn as if it were really a church of some kind, and as I remember how it always made me feel I really can't imagine any difference.

In the far corner where the wall met the first stall was where Spencer would have set up the tree that late the day before he had cut and drug down from somewhere off the high ridge that looks over the lower part of the ranch. Lonny went with him on horseback, and watching from the parlor window we saw them walking their horses out of the growing dark with Lonny's horse first and Spencer's a step or two behind with the tree tied off at his saddlehorn and dragging over the surface of the snow.

And I remember the candles. The whole tree seemed full of lit candles. So many of them that their light seemed to push back the darkness when we'd come into the barn from out of the hard cold black night. And the shocking pristine vision of that candlelight would be like a miracle to me when I'd first see it. And then I'd see that all amongst the candles were hung apples and carrots and other fruits and vegetables wherever the broad boughs of the tree would support them.

Haybales would be positioned on the earthen floor for places to sit in front of the tree and also to separate the two or three horses, all groomed and with a tiny red or green knot of ribbon tied in their forelocks, who were free to walk about on the other side where Spencer had placed hay and grain for them to eat. Several yearling calves would be settled in two of the stalls and a number of weanling lambs that Spencer had trucked over from Ollie Wheeler's early that morning in two others.

Toebowman would be sitting on one of the bales and playing and humming along as he picked at the strings of his instrument with those gloves that leave the fingertips exposed. We thought he'd cut off the ends of his gloves so he'd be able to play his guitar in the cold, and I remember thinking about cutting the ends of my mittens too but seemed to forget before actually getting it done. There'd be platters of cookies and pitchers of juice for the kids and eggnog for the folks and glasses arranged on trays that were set on top of three bales that were piled one on the other against the near wall.

The kids'd break away from the folks and the folks'd cluster on either side of Toebowman with handshakes all around and all the good wishes spoken back and forth from out of that shared existence of people living close enough to the earth to be kin to the various other families of beings who lived there also in that harsh and generally unforgiving environment that made us all—the Bowmans the next ranch over and nearly four miles away, and Ollie Wheeler and his family and hands and their families nearly fifteen miles off to the south—all neighbors. Folks who worked much longer hours than their work-animals, from dark to dark and most always beyond, day after day without heed of arbitrary divisions of time into weeks or months, and so telling the passage of it by the building and diminishing of the light and the waxing and waning of the moon and perhaps too by the awesome concentric circles of the fiery and yearning stars.

And closer to the heart, by the births and deaths of all the creatures given and taken from life around and about our high clear place on the earth that was rimmed by the near hills on one side and the far mountains on the other. Winged and two- and four-legged and silver swimmers and arrowlike flyers and runners horned and not with cloven feet and some with ten toes. The peach-fuzz turning to whiskers on the sons of man and coming up from the barn some warm Saturday evening seeing the gangly little girl you'd known right from seed suddenly appearing on the porch like her own lovely ghost waiting and then hugging you around your neck that had to still smell of the horse you'd been shoeing and saying, Your supper'll be cold Daddy. And kissing her cheek, a woman, with her mother in her eyes and her own daughter there too if you were wise enough to see that far. And time turning grey in your beard and your hands like limp old claws turned hard with callus and age and your fingers cracking in the deathlike cold and healing with the earth under the healed places and cracking open again like fissures in the frozen ground waiting for the renewal of spring to restore what is held in abeyance back to the tender and fecund flesh, another winter. For time here wasn't generally referred to in years but rather in the winters we have lived through. The sun is low and the warmth is brief and the light lives on between the dark and the dark.

Toebowman would be singing softly at first so that we hadn't really been paying that much attention until one by one the grownups would join in as their kids seemed to gravitate back up against them with their young wild voices catching a word here and there and making up others as their folks sang along. And one or two of the ranchers droning with one fixed tone that probably sounded to them as if they were warbling away with everyone else. A joining of voices in that delicate light that somehow seemed to generate a warmth, a suspiration of living breath and a real warmth that was undeniable. As if each of the creatures that lay or stood or sat in that drafty close place made enough of a contribution to the engendered atmosphere to actually produce a living heat from out of the barren cold that pressed against the outside walls.

Then Spencer would take out his spectacles and set them low on his nose and sit in front of the tree so that its light fell onto the children's book that he held with both hands and always read from about the Baby and the animals, and how the animals were all given human speech on this one night. And as I listened I remembered that I planned to get up later so I could get dressed and get my boots on and come back down to the barn to hear what each of the horses and dogs and cats and the cattle and sheep would sound like when they spoke actual words. Wondering what they would say to each other, but especially what they would say to me when I spoke to them. And Whitney looks at me from the corner of his eye so I know he's thinking the same thing.

But we wake up much later than we should have, and Whitney's already dressing himself as I rush to catch up to him. And he whispers fiercely, Pa said they do it at midnight. And as I'm trying to get my flannel nightshirt tucked into my jeans I say, Maybe they're still doing it because it's still dark outside. And then we bump and shush each other down the stairs as we hold on to the railing.

The cold freezes the inside of my nose, it's so cold, and I breathe into the collar of my jacket. The stars are like little white holes all across the black sky and Sirius, all aglimmer with red and blue and white light too, hangs just above the roof of the barn as we slide the door open just enough to squeeze through and then close it behind us. But we're too late. Lemon comes up to me in the dark and noses into my fingers but he doesn't say anything even when I rub his head against my chest and say, Hi Lemon. Hi Lemon. And I know how his mouth smiles when I scratch his ears but he still doesn't speak. At least not with words anyway.

I turn the light on in the tackroom and leave the door open so the light spreads out across the dark runway. And then I hear Whitney over by Blue's stall, standing on a haybale and speaking softly to him with Blue's head lifted and his legs folded under him and his gentle eyes blinking against our intrusion. Hi Blue, Whitney says. Hi Blue. And I climb up behind him and watch the horse's face as he continues to blink into wakefulness with his lovely pale eyelashes.

We can hear other animals in their stalls restive in the darkness and groaning with sleep, and one of them drinking while another one whinnies softly as if to itself, instantly reminding me then in memory as well as now how I've loved the voice of horses for my entire life. It's too late, I whisper to Whitney shaking my head. We got here too late. And Whitney whispers back, I know but next year we have to remember. And I whisper back at him, Yes we have to remember. Next year.

Toebowman always plays *Silent Night* last, maybe three or four times in a row, and everybody knows the words and sings it with him. And the seeming perfection of those simple sounds, with all the people huddled together warm out of the vast cold and safe somehow out of the vast dark, makes me feel as if the beauty that I didn't then know the word for was nearly too big to hold all at once. And so for a moment I have to stop singing so I can swallow two or three times before I can make the song begin again.

I'm leaning against Elizabeth's legs as she sets against Spencer sitting on a couple of haybales with Whitney leaning against his legs and against me, and Lonny on Spencer's other side with Spencer's arm around him and his other hand resting on Whitney's shoulder, and Elizabeth's arm around Spencer's back and her other hand resting over my chest. And by the time we come to the Sleep-in-heavenly-peace line, her hand lifts off me and rises up and then settles back so that I can see her face again in my mind and even know the water in her eyes slipping over her cheeks like quicksilver in the candlelight without having to turn and look up at her. And her hand goes off me again and then comes back, and I don't have to look at it either because I know how it looks in my mind too just as I know her face.

And besides I can't take my eyes off the candles, how wondrous a vision they are to me with their fragile light that for some reason makes me think of how aspen leaves tremble when the wind blows into them. And so perhaps if those leaves were to magically be transformed into something else, they'd become candlelight too because aspen leaves and candlelight both seem to tremble and quiver in just exactly the same way.

Sleep I think for all the massed days and clicking years of my tiny flickering life. Sleep I think of Spencer whose soul parties with the antelope smelling of sage and horselather and covered by the insubstantial globe of a great tumbleweed. Sleep I think of Elizabeth who glides over the sea with her long yellow hair trailing above the dim dark monument of the endless turning tide. Sleep I think of Lonny who bears his gentleness like a food to be offered to anyone who approaches him hungry for it or not.

And sleep I think to myself for all of us for all of

us beating fiercely against the wind or lying placidly beneath its cool touch with broken hands and wondrous wings and blinded eyes that see even beyond seeing the same wordless dream built of the same heartcrushing sorrow and the same unspeakable loveliness all at the same time how beautiful and sad it is all at the same time.

    And sleep i think for all of us sleep i think at last
oh sleep in heavenly peace
sleep

II

HANDS

We'd been feeding the cattle off horse-drawn sleds, which is how it'd always been done in our country, Luke says. Big wooden platforms on runners with a two-by-four frame front and back to pile the haybales against, and each sled pulled by one of our two teams of Belgian drafthorses. Massive two-thousand-pound animals with thick winter coats and huge shaggy feet and a manner as gentle as their bodies were strong.

And Whitney and I would have to help before going to school. Spencer would get us up in the dark and half-asleep we'd dress against the cold and then meet him in the barn where he and Red, our foreman, would already be graining the horses. And then one of us would go with one of them. One day I'd be with Spencer and Whitney with Red, and the next day we'd switch off, day after day after day.

But this was the morning after New Year's and Red and Aggie, his wife, had stayed at their daughter's near Rawlins for the holidays and Spencer had told him to take an extra day or two. The snow was blowing sideways and the temperature against the outside of the barn read minus twenty-eight and of course it was still dark. We took one team, working just the one sled, for Spencer would feed off the other one after we came back and Whitney and I had to leave. And even though Spencer would be by himself, at least he'd have the dawn by then.

The horses strain in their traces until the runners under the loaded sled break free with a sharp crack from where they've set overnight and frozen to the earthen floor, and then we move out into the blizzard and away from the shelter of the outbuildings. The horses know the way by sight or not, and once they enter the meadow Spencer ties the reins around one of the forward posts on the sled and then kneels down where Whitney and I are huddled amongst the bales. When we start out it's still night although the relentless flat wall of snow that races by us begins to gain some subtle gradation of what could only be perceived as notdarkness. The horses continue to prow ahead with their terrific slow inexorability until the bawling cattle begin to materialize as from behind an almost solid-seeming grey curtain. And so we can hear the animals approaching for a time before we can actually see them.

Spencer cuts and pulls and then wraps the twine that holds each bale as Whitney and I begin to cast the hay down off the sled, dividing each long rectangular block roughly into thirds that we let drop on the snow as cattle follow closely behind us and then fall back. Whitney soon begins to fling his flakes of hay almost in a rage of cold and I know how he feels because there are times when it all seems like it's more than a man should be asked to endure. When it's so cold that it seems like you're losing more than you could ever hope to gain, and the harder you try the more you just seem to fall behind.

We continue to crawl along ahead of the interminable crush of cattle, the near faces of hungry animals parting and beginning to eat as other animals move in to take their places, endlessly. Whitney throws his arm again as I bend to another bale and I think I hear him cry out in the shrieking wind but I can't be sure, even though he's only just an arm's length away. And then for some reason he suddenly kneels down with his gloved hand against his chest and he screams something into the wind again that I still can't hear as I turn and toss the hay in a continuous repetition that I seemingly cannot stop. And then after another moment Whitney rises back up and begins again.

The horses draw the sled with that same plodding nonprogress even after the load of hay has all been distributed. Spencer sits with us with our backs against the front cross-member of the frame, facing away from the great round rumps of the two Belgians and huddled into the collars of our coats with our gloved hands thrust into our pockets. Dawn is on the snow at last but with hardly any light at all as if the two drafthorses pull us into a colorless windtunnel where the knifing blizzard continues without alteration except in terms of visibility. Although there is nothing to see except the snow horizonless and with no point of reference to mark where the earth ends or the sky begins.

And then as we finally approach the entrance to the meadow again, the opening in the fenceline, Spencer gets back up and unties the reins and guides the animals who know exactly where they are going whether he stands with them or not. Far off and higher up the barn's lights sail behind the streaming storm illuminating next to nothing and obviously making no impression whatsoever on that iron-grey shroud of opaque darkness that must be the new day. Stillborn.

Whitney and I sit against each other's arms as Spencer stands above us with one leg alongside my shoulder. We hump our backs against the cold but there is no escape, for the cold will have its way. The hollow sun wherever it is has no warmth left to give and even if it dared to show itself it seems as if it probably must have used up all of its fiery essence a long time ago. And so only the wind is left to cleave the world as it will, paring away the fragile warmblooded creatures as with a surgeon's scalpel until the flesh feels as if it's been laid bare. The wind as both tormentor and redeemer too when you finally surrender to it, when you finally cross over from the near agony of sentience to a state almost of unconcern, for when the cold goes so deep as to defeat itself it just doesn't make any difference anymore. Almost like death. For only death can defeat death.

Then we're finally back in the barn and Spencer's on the other side of the team at their harness and I'm carrying a sack of grain over to the bin which has been fed down low. Several lightbulbs try to lessen the darkness but it's so cold that their light seems frozen about them, little pools of brightness that hover like halos beneath their reflectors but doing little to change that perpetual dusk as we go about our chores, the cold slogging blood that won't warm and fingers too numb to feel what they need to touch.

I begin to turn with my load when Whitney suddenly flings a grain-bucket at an empty stall. The near drafthorse flicks the skin along its jaw as if responding to imaginary insects but still stands stolidly beside the other animal that doesn't move at all and with Spencer still at its cheekstrap. I hear Spencer say, Huh? as Whitney yells, It's too fucking cold to live here. And then he kicks at the pail that's bounded back at him so it glances off the stall partition and ricochets off the little window with a spiderweb now cracked in its surface. This time the horses do flinch taking a half-step to the side as the animal that Spencer holds in harness moves its great head away from the clatter of the bucket.

One moment Spencer's on the other side of the team and the next without seeming to have even moved, his gloved fist is under Whitney's chin driving him up against the wall and holding him off his feet by the front of his coat so that Spencer's face is nearly touching Whitney's, with Whitney's eyes showing all their white like a horse's does when it's frightened and Spencer's face a hard white rage that we had never seen before, as if all the blood had left it to give even more strength to his arm and hand that hold Whitney pinned against the wall as if he were made of straw beneath his heavy winter coat instead of a young man of probably at that time a hundred and thirty or forty pounds.

Cold? Spencer says in that low seething rage. Did I hear you say something about the cold? And Whitney with the fear in his eyes but with his youthful defiance still intact cries, It's fucking ridiculous living like this almost freezing to death and the cattle almost freezing. That number 76 cow. My hand cracked against her head and her goddamn ear broke off. Her ear broke off! he screams. With the ear-tag still in it. And he can do nothing to stop the tears springing down his face with Spencer's eyes only inches away and burning through him like an incandescent white flame.

That's lucky that's all she lost, Spencer says. You think this is cold? I'll tell you what cold is. Because this is a fucking walk in the park. You hear me? This is a fucking walk in the park. I'll tell you what cold is. Cold is seventeen years ago to the day yesterday morning. Cold is what we call Cemetery Ridge on New Year's morning and I don't know what the Germans called it but I've got seven men left out of fifty and half of them deaf or bleeding from their ears from the artillery that's been pounding us for three days and when dawn comes so it's still dark on the snow we can hear the Germans before we can see them and I run up to my point-men who're hunkered over their machine-guns where they've been sleeping and I bang them awake because the Germans are pouring over that ridge pouring hard and coming down and I Bang on Tullio on one point and I Bang on Gallagher my second point. And each time he says "bang" he drives Whitney even harder up against the wooden planking. And Gallagher mumbles something that I don't hear because I'm already banging on Dickinson who is barely eighteen years old who has been here for three months who has a girlfriend whose picture he showed me who is still in high school in Spring-fucking-Hill Maine who put his hand out and shook mine six hours ago at the stroke of midnight and who I said to along with the others Let's pray to God that we don't have to spend another New Year's in this hellhole. And it's Dickinson who starts singing *Silent Night* so all of us are singing it with him whether we ever been to a church or not. And Dickinson who has red hair and still has freckles Dickinson won't wake up and I scream Come on Howie and I can hear the Germans and I can hear someone beside me saying They're coming they're coming and Dickinson is frozen like a goddamn statue. His eyes are frozen open and he's frozen against his Browning .30-

fucking-caliber air-cooled machine-gun and I need his weapon. My men need his weapon and so I start hacking away at his hands. I've got tears in my eyes and I'm screaming at myself and I'm screaming that this man is dead and I'm hacking his hands off. I've got my bayonet into his hands and I've cut and I've cut and I've cut and I can't get through the bone and so I'm stomping on his arms with my boot to break his hands free so I can get somebody on his weapon. I'm stomping on his arms until they finally break away but his hands are still frozen in the handles of that Browning and so I'm prying at his fingers with the tip of my bayonet. His mittens are all slashed away and the fingers the frozen tendons like white knots are frozen in the handles and I'm prying them away. I'm digging under his fingers that don't want to let go. That just won't let go.

So cold, he says almost in a whisper and with a weariness that makes it sound as if it were not him anymore but his very soul that was talking. We're all cold, he says, with Whitney back on the ground by then so he stands as if at attention. We're all cold, Spencer says. And we all still have both of our two hands too. And so if you're cold you can go on up to the house. Now. But I don't want to hear about it. Do you understand?

And then that night lying in the dark in our beds and whispering back and forth because Whitney and I had never heard our father use a real cussword before, the "damns" and the "shits" maybe but nothing that'd get you thrown out of a class for it. But then when we thought about it we understood that there was nothing that could be said, there was no word or string of words that a body could come up with that could in any way free someone of the memories that Spencer had had to live with. And that we in turn would now share with him for the rest of our own time unforgotten along with our own yet-to-be-discovered trials and misfortunes that are part and parcel of each and every one of us who tries to get through this life on just two legs. As if that awful and enduring gut-ache of human sorrow was just the going market-price for having the pride and presumption to think that with all the other creatures who needed all four legs to make it through on, that you could get'er done on just the two.

And seeming to see clearly for one moment before it all clouded up again and slipped back into that vast obscurity of question and doubt, I suddenly saw how each life's joy and pain were made just exactly right for that life so that they fit that life perfectly like its own skin. And so no other body could possibly get in and try it on for itself because every other body had its own perfect skin too.

And the more you could stand the more you'd be given, so you were always filled right up to your own personal limit where one more drop, which you could count on, would push it over the edge. And so you would somehow have to find the way to contain it too, that one drop too many, and maybe just to see how much you could actually bear. And whether your capacity be a thimbleful or the whole damn ocean, the well of your precious collected humor be it tears today or your life's blood tomorrow will surely drown the fragile flame of your existence given the addition of that inevitable next drop. Unless you grow. Unless you become big enough to still hold it all.

And so like it or not, you would learn what you were given the breath of life to learn. You would learn what you unknowingly came here to learn. And your sorrow and grief and your joys and pleasures too would teach you your lessons in a curriculum devised just precisely for you. The man who spends his life chasing golden rings for his naked and grasping fingers, and the man who mourns his fingers with rings of gold in careless abundance but no hands to put them on.

PASSAGES

When my mare died, Luke says, the day we put my mare down. I hadn't been able to ride her for over a year because her back had gotten so bad. And Spencer had told me that she would have to be put down someday because eventually the pain would just be too much for her. You could run your hand along her backbone and feel the muscle wince up as you passed over these arthritic edges that had grown there. Until finally she could hardly lie down nor stand back up again. I'd go into her stall and she'd move back and forth from off one foot onto the other trying to find one position of relative neutrality that maybe would hurt her a little less. And so I finally had to admit to myself that leaving her like that was more cruel than the alternative.

Spencer was away on business and I'd gone down to the barn to grain her early one Saturday morning, humping my shoulders up at how cold it was right at the beginning of October. And I remember cutting more corn into her feed for the heat we'd been taught was generated digestively or something, and so I emptied the bucket of it into her trough and then took some of it in my hand as she began to move over to that side of the stall. I put my arm across her withers speaking to her as she nuzzled the grain off my open palm and she nickered deep down in her throat. And I remember watching her great gentle eyes as I spoke to her until it suddenly hit me as if she'd spun around and nailed me, it suddenly hit me as I talked to her eyes just how much pain she was in. And all the while she kept mincing from one foot to the other as she continued to sidle her way over to the grain trough.

So I storm back through the kitchen past Whitney who's still at the table eating and reading his sports-page, and looking up at me as I'm dialing the phone, he says, What is it? I look in his eyes as the line opens and I say, Stony? And Whitney keeps watching me with his

spoon in his bowl as I ask our vet, Stony Walls, if he
could come over that morning for my mare. Which was
our mother's horse that she'd raised from a foal. And I
say, I think she's just hurting too bad anymore. And
Stony says he'll be over right around nine o'clock.

I sit down at the table with my own bowl and pour
out some of the breakfast food and Whitney asks, What
time? I tell him and he buries himself back in his paper
while I try to eat, staring out the window as morning
comes on bleak and grey. And then Whitney says without looking up, Today? And I answer him without looking back from the window, Today.

I go back down to the barn and soon I hear Whitney
start up the backhoe and chug away, and then as it begins
to run smoother and quieter its sound fades down
toward the meadow. The mare's still eating at the trough
and I bring her a bucket of fresh water so she looks up
from the grain and drinks and then goes back to her feed
as I begin to brush her down. And I work over her
slowly, remembering her through all the years of my life,
with the winter hair already on her. And all the while the
sound of her eating in the dim emptiness of the barn is a
peace to both of us. I rub my free hand over her following my other hand with the brush and then comb her
long thick tail and finally her mane too. And for a mo-

ment she stops the grinding in her jaws and turns and just looks at me and then bows her head over the grain once again.

I run my hand down her leg and kneel beneath her and then lay each leg in turn across my thigh so I can clean her hooves. She hadn't had shoes on in over a year since we'd stopped working her, and I remember thinking how good her feet looked all trimmed up even and all. My lifting her feet troubled her though for she continued to shift back and forth and from side to side, and so I worked quickly letting her lean her weight against my shoulder.

There's a white Y-shaped scar between the second and third knuckles of my left hand that runs into the webbing between those two fingers that reminds me of a day a couple of years ago when we were out looking for strays and somehow ended up all the way over into Whiskey Basin where I'd never been before. We come out of the timber just at dusk and there's an old settler's cabin down below and I know we need to be getting back. But instead we keep on across the abandoned pasture that's all gone to sage and scrub oak and past the corral that's twisted over and buried in the tall grass beside the fallen-down barn. Until we approach the disused ranchhouse with the evening star, Venus I think it was, hanging just above the caved-in roof. And with all the windows poked out too like some old veteran of some ancient war still dressed in the tattered faded remnants of his uniform and with his skeleton's eyesockets staring and lifeless.

And I knew I should have dismounted and led the mare on foot in case there was wire somewhere that I couldn't see, but it was late and I told myself she'd be alright. But I knew even before she stepped between two of the old rotted fenceposts that I was wrong. She steps again and begins to lift that hoof out of the dust and the refuse of decayed leaves, and time somehow seems to slow down almost to a standstill. And so her right forefoot begins to come away from the darkening ground, and with it a careless loop of barbed-wire that's snared about her fetlock. And as that hoof lifts higher than it should for the next step she begins coming back on her hind legs slowly and slowly so the front of her reaches even higher still and paws at the dark sky as if she were trying to touch Venus which by then shines as bright as a miniature moon. And as I'm trying to coax her with infinite care come girl come girl ahead and down with my voice and my spurs, she overpasses her balance and tumbles backward with a shriek of fright as I crash down too. With her on top of me.

She rolls across me and as my body turns in the dust

I sense her arcing high above me shrieking again at
Venus and at that dark barbed stubbornness at her foot
that still won't let go. And waiting and waiting but where
she finally breaks herself free and falls back to earth. And
waiting and waiting but where the steel-shod hoof as
final as nightfall comes crashing down on my hand my
left hand and the force of it seems to throw me just half
again in the red but tasteless dust leaving only an echoing
silence that dims to black. Until however later I don't
know when I feel the reins that must have fallen over her
head brushing past my face, and then the soft skin of her
muzzle and lips as she nibbles at the ground where I lie
seeking my touch.

I'd finished my grooming and she her eating, and uncon-
sciously I glance again at that scar between my fingers as
I fasten her halter and then lead her out into the dull
morning. We walk far down the knoll that fronts the
ranch along the creek and she drinks again and then we
move back along the rising slope where we can drop
down through the dense wood and into the clearing.
Whitney's machine was quiet by then and I knew he had
finished. He'd meet Stony back at the house and'd take
him down to the meadow in the old uncovered jeep
that'd also been there as long as I can remember.

The trees are all bare, naked white trees that rise all

around us, and we walk across a silent carpet of mottled golden leaves as we pass through the wood. It's still real cold and the breath-vapor puffs out from both of us as I walk beside her with the leadrope slack in my hand as if she knows where we're headed, although I know it is really just the downgoing of the hillside. We finally come out of the trees at the far side of the clearing for I had glimpsed the backhoe and so have taken us the long way around as if we were trying to evade some mortal force that awaited us with a great yellow arm, which indeed we were. I walk up against her so her cheek brushes against my arm as we go. I know they're waiting for us across the field but I'm having a difficult time turning back towards them and so we keep walking further and further away in the direction of the barn and home.

We have walked enough so that her stride has evened out and she seems to move without any lameness at all and I dwell on her familiar innocent face as it swings up against me with her step. As we approach the rise of the hill that climbs up to the lowest corral I will myself to turn away and we move quickly back towards where the jeep and the machine are parked and where the two men await us. Whitney comes over to me as I approach and takes the leadrope from my hand and moves a few steps off with the mare as she begins grazing. Stony is leaning against the jeep and begins to fix a syringe with the contents of a vial that he's taken from his jacket.

Stony, I say. And he says, Mornin Luke. I'm awful sorry. And the way he says "awful" goes straight through me as I look at him working with his gear and I'm reminded of what a kind and gentle man he is behind all his gruffness, and that for all the years I've known him I have never seen him be harsh with an animal. I suddenly hate the look of his instrument though and without looking up he says, It's the best way son. You know me and your pap come from the old school of getting things done, but this is the best way. She'll just kneel down in the grass and then lie over and be done with it.

And I say, Just as long as it's quick enough so it won't be a hurt to her. And he says, Don't you worry son. This here is enough for two animals her size and I'm giving her all of it. If'n she feels anything at all it'll be the first moment in all this time when she wasn't hurting.

Whitney brings her alongside the deep slash he's dug in the raw earth with the backhoe and hands me the leadrope. And I'm holding her face against me, my fingers under the straps of the headstall and my thumbs rubbing at the soft corners of her mouth which was something she always liked. Stony moves next to her and rubs his left hand flat along the length of her neck and suddenly jabs the needle that he's holding with his other hand into the vein that runs there, and there's a bright instant of blood that he closes off with the syringe. Then he depresses the plunger and almost immediately one of her forelegs starts to bend as I keep her great head against me trying to hold her upright even as she crumbles under me and rolls onto her side with her legs facing the hole.

Stony kneels down and feels at her chest and says, She's gone boys. Her heart'll beat on for a few more moments but it'll just be the reflex. Whitney kneels down and replaces Stony's hand with his as Stony stands back up and says, I'm gonna run up to my vehicle. I meant to bring a scalpel to dissect the top of her backbone, see what that actually looks like, least if you boys don't mind. And Whitney says, It's still beating. And I say, No, I don't guess it'd make any goddamn difference now anyway. And so Stony gets in the jeep and goes off.

I kneel down next to Whitney and he moves aside and I lay my hand up against her and feel her heart beating raggedly within her. I watch at her dead face with her eyelid nearly closed and she groans and so I stay there on my knees. And her heart which had been racing against the inevitability of the poison seems to ease into a slower rhythm and so I say to Whitney, She's goin now. It's slowin down now. But it keeps on with a dull and steady persistence until she suddenly takes in a great inhalation of air and lets it back out and I say, Jesus, out loud to myself. And Whitney says, What? And I say, She's still alive, Whitney. And he shakes his head and says, You heard him, Luke, it's just the reflex. And I say, I swear to Christ, Whitney. And he kneels down beside me as she breathes again and presses his hand under mine and says, Goddamnit. And then standing back up, Where the Fuck is he?

The jeep is finally audible coming off the hill and as I watch her, her eyelid rises enough for me to see her living pupil. And I'm repeating over and over inside myself, I'm sorry I'm sorry. And her heartbeat is slow and steady in her breast which is still warm against my hand.

Whitney has gone past the backhoe as Stony drives up and Whitney yells, She ain't dead, Stony. And so Stony comes and kneels down where I am and I stand back up and he injects her again and this time stays against her until there is an absolute nullity where his hand lies. I kneel at her head and move her eyelid back down and then lift her face so I can move the halter around where I can unfasten it.

And I think now she is free. Now there is nothing to hold her back. And I let her go.

LOVE

He could hear the August wind again, and then broken and quiet and then perfectly clear the clash of hay machinery from the field down below and for one instant Spencer's voice calling, Where in the blazes did Luke go? Who at that moment, fugitive and on foot and having already turned all the bales on the ground in advance of whoever was driving the flatbed which was still a whole pasture away, had apparently disappeared. And wondering if she'd be there as they had planned and before he had to return to his chores, when Luke finally did climb up and over the ridge, she was already running towards him.

And then the warm wind must have changed again because there was only the sound of the dry rustling grass rubbing together beneath golden tassels that waved and bowed over them while her skin under his hand made a flame in him that he could hardly stand, her fingers locked about his wrist where his pulse ran crashing in his ears and pounding in his chest.

They both must have fallen asleep, wearied by the force and heat of the blood risen so precipitously that it carried them right up to that line that still wouldn't be crossed. And then they woke to the noise of more machinery that sounded as if it were nearly right below them once again the way the wind carries sound sometimes so you can hear voices or an animal or a bird as if they were nearby when in fact they were actually some distance away. And almost with that same facility that sometimes makes time and distance seem nearly interchangeable, so you could swear you'd been someplace before that you were seeing for the first time. Or maybe in truth, just seeing with new eyes.

He could hear Whitney's voice this time over the clashing noise and then it was quiet again. She sat up and turned around to button her blouse while Luke sat up too and brought his t-shirt back over his head saying, I guess, the way Red always said "I guess" when it was time to go back to work. But just as his face reemerged she pushed him back against the ground crushing her mouth against his. And then she was gone.

When he finally climbed up behind the tractor that Whitney was driving, standing on the axle and catching the back of Whitney's seat with his hand, Whitney turns and shakes his head and then turns back around and raising his voice says, You got your lip all busted. And still running his tongue across the place where she had marked him, Luke climbs off the rack that holds the hayrake and jumping down strides across to where more finished bales are spaced haphazardly on the new-mown ground and begins turning and straightening them so they'll be ready to be bucked up onto the flatbed when it comes. And that was a day's workout that easily surpassed anything you could make up in the gym. Ten and sometimes twelve hours a day, and day after day, until the hay was all in. Which usually took the better part of at least a couple of months.

That was the summer before their senior year and the football team was practicing in the evenings under the lights because everyone else was haying during the day too. Even the kids from town, even they were working on someone's hay crew. And it had been a good summer for both the hay and the team. And they knew they were going to be good. You could just feel it when they came out of the lockerroom because there was something almost kinetic, almost explosive, in the way they took the field. Almost as if the violence of practice and then of scrimmage released like a nightly catharsis the harsh sum of the highland sun in their backs and shoulders and the hard stiff labor of the day that still formed their hands. And so it seemed that if they just put in enough time and gained enough repetition so the patterns and the plays became natural responses or really instinctive reactions rather than problems to solve, which in the physical world gets you there a step too late, then they just might have something.

So it was a good summer. And the team started off good too. They won the first six games and then lost the next one on a fumbled punt when they ran out of time before they could score again, although they were knocking on the door when the game ended. Then the following weekend they had to travel all the way across the state to Plainview, a perennial powerhouse and state champions the last two years. And it started to snow before the end of the first quarter and never stopped.

Luke went up as high as he could and somehow came down with Percy's pass which had led him a little too far but he was still able to hang on. He remembered it hitting the fingertips of his right hand and as he flew into it getting his other hand on it too and drawing it against his chest just as the defender racing across and almost out of control with the poor footing caught him with a knee to his side before he hit the ground.

He still had the ball under him and two opponents on top of him and he couldn't breathe. He tried to say something but nothing came out and when they finally got off him he still couldn't breathe. He could sneak a little air in through his teeth but that was about all because it felt like he had a knife stuck in his side, and when he tried to inhale it seemed to go into him even further. They got him taken off the field and then to the hospital where they saw on the films that he'd broken two ribs on his right side. The same two, the doctor said, that he could see had been broken sometime before.

Jerry D'Angelo, the equipment manager and Carl the trainer's assistant, went with him and brought his clothesbag too and so after they x-rayed him and showed him the fractures they let him take a shower before taping him up. He sneezed while he was drying himself and went down on one knee clutching the edge of the table that set against the wall and holding on to it until he could finally unclench his teeth. He still couldn't really get a good breath of air but the taping somehow helped, and so after he was sufficiently bound up he could breathe again almost normally.

He wanted to go back to the game and was there for the last few minutes. The field was all covered with snow and they had kids on both sidelines with big janitor's brooms pushing it toward the benches so you could see where the yard-lines came up to the little yellow markers that had the yardage numbers on them. They won by six points and Whitney got the game-ball. He was all over the field and they later heard that he'd broken the state record for the most tackles in one game. He also picked up a blocked kick in the fourth quarter and took it into the endzone, losing his feet and sliding on his stomach for the last five yards he said before three of the other team jumped on top of him like he was a pile of leaves or a snowbank or something.

Luke was still in the hospital and so he missed Whitney's touchdown. When he did return, without his pads but with the heavy windbreaker over him and still wearing his helmet to keep the snow off, Whitney put his hand on Luke's shoulder and shook his head when Luke told him it was those same two ribs that he'd broken a couple of years before. But even worse was that he wouldn't be able to play in their last two games. And so that was that. Whitney gave him the trophy ball later when they were getting ready to get on the bus, but Luke shook his head and said, All I did was break some ribs. Whitney said, You and me both know that that ain't quite all of it, but you can hold on to it for Pa then. And so Whitney took Luke's equipment bag for him and Luke carried the ball.

The folks from the other school had gotten together a bunch of food in cartons that were already stacked up on the bus when they came out of the lockerroom. They'd invited them to stay with their families for the night until the storm passed but a couple of state troopers who were down on the field had told the coach and Darrell their busdriver that once they left the flat open country where the game was it sounded like it was beginning to lighten up and so they should be OK if they were still determined to go.

It was wild on the bus with the players and coaches and cheerleaders all laughing and talking at the top of their voices and eating at the same time. And Denny Reid, the head coach, coming up and down the aisle and sitting for a minute in any temporarily vacant seat to say something to whoever happened to be sitting next to him. Luke kept trying to find a way to position himself that would maybe back off the pain in his side some, but when the coach approached Whitney got up so he could sit down.

There was still some of that hardness from the disagreement the coach and the two boys had had the year before, but that was water under the bridge and as good as the team was doing this year the three of them were bound and without anything actually being said that personal feelings weren't going to get in the way of what they wanted to accomplish. Which was the state championship. Which was after Thanksgiving. And for which a little mountain town from the western part of the state, like Lewiston, had never contended. Until now.

And too, whatever else that had come up between them there had always been an abiding respect for who each of them were, the Davis boys on one side and the coach on the other. He was a good coach and they were good players and whatever choices they'd had to make between their responsibilities to their family's ranch and the team, whether the coach disagreed with them or not, had never once called into question the indisputable fact that they had been two of the better kids that he'd ever had—hardnosed and unflinching and with that natural athleticism that had jumped out at him the first time he ever saw them. And he admired them too however grudgingly and knew when they moved on that as much as he ever allowed himself such a luxury, he would miss them. He knew too that he would probably never let them know, but he knew it would be so.

He had two blankets with him that he placed next to

Luke who was partially turned in his seat with his arms crossed on his chest. The coach had a water-bottle too and a little tin of pills that he held out when he sat down. Aspirin, he says. Carl says to take a couple now and then two more in three or four hours when these start to wear off. Luke turns and takes the water and two of the pills and says, Thanks Coach. Then he gathers up the blankets and begins to wedge them between himself and the wall of the bus. The coach gets up and touches his arm and says, If it gets bad come up front and get Carl. Hear? Thanks Coach, Luke says again, and then rests back as the coach moves on to his next charge.

Gets bad? Luke presses off the lights over his and Whitney's seats and readjusts the blankets until he finds a position that seems to bother him least and then closes his eyes. Whitney never did come back and so Luke half-lies and half-sits with part of his outside leg resting against the edge of the adjoining seat. Eventually it got quiet and most of the bus was dark. There was a light on a few rows ahead where someone was reading and then all the way up front where the coach and the trainer sat in the first row.

Maybe he fell asleep or maybe he was still awake, he couldn't remember, but a hand passed behind his shoulder and touched his neck and she whispered against his jaw, was he warm enough. The blanket that he'd had about him had fallen away and when he turned from the window so he was sitting upright he was more in Whitney's seat than in his own. She hushed him before he spoke, getting past his bent knees and bringing another blanket with her so she could lean against the wall and the window where he had originally positioned himself. When she was finally settled she put her arm around his shoulders drawing him into her so the blanket she had brought draped around both of them. He eased himself against her with the side of his face at the top of her chest and his folded hands in her lap with her other hand lain over them. Her arm that was around him seemed to fold him in as he rested against her so he somehow felt small even though he could feel the bulk of his shoulder as she held it.

There was a time when the bus jumped and then came down hard as if they had flown across a pothole or something in the road. And his hand had clutched her arm as it had the table edge in the hospital room when he went down on his knee, until the thing that felt like a knife in his side finally subsided, and then lapsing back in the darkness and slowly burning itself out letting him rest his hand down again with his other hand that she still held. Her fingers that had dug into his shoulder as if she would replace what hurt him with the catlike tenacity of her grip when he groaned and grabbed her arm, loosened at last and she hushed him again and brought that hand away and with it stroked his neck and then kissed him there. When she fell asleep still holding him like that her lips still rested on his skin.

They never even made it back to the state highway, which had been closed anyway because of blowing and drifting snow, and they could see how bad it was in the flashing lights of the troopers' patrol car that was parked at the bottom of the exit. They all sat upright and watched out the windows. Sometime earlier she had returned to her seat and Whitney was beside him once again. The whole bus was awake and the noise of voices grew back gradually almost to the level of where it had left off after they had finished eating. Even at a crawl the bus slid sideways for several feet before coming to a stop. One of the troopers walked up to Darrell's window while the other one continued to wave vehicles away from the blocked-off entrance ramp.

The overhead lights came back on and the coach stood up and took a few steps toward the center of the bus and called out that they'd have to find someplace to stay. The bus was moving again and the coach went back and sat down as they proceeded toward what appeared to be a bright cloud down on the ground and up ahead that was actually the lights of the next town diffused by the heavy curtain of the falling snow. It wasn't but about ten-thirty on Saturday night and it had taken them nearly four hours to travel less than eighty-five miles and they still hadn't even really begun their journey home, which needed the barricaded westbound highway to get them to the other side of the state.

They pulled into a gas-station directly off the road. There'd already been more than two feet of snow since that afternoon and it was still coming down and blowing so hard that the little cash-and-carry store on the far side of the lot was nearly invisible from the two pump islands where they parked.

Three or four of the players sprang up from their seats and started down the aisle but the coach motioned them back, saying, Let's find someplace to stay and then we'll all get off together. He turned and went back up front and then got down off the bus himself and went across to a lone phone-booth that stood bleakly against a wall of tall hedges all piled up with snow. And then a few minutes later he came back under Darrell's window presumably for more pocket-change. When he got back on the bus and they were moving again, they soon turned onto a long strip that was all motels and fast-food shops, and a cheer went up in the bus.

The first place they came to had two parallel rows of

little log cabins set back from the road and as they pulled up in front the neon "Vacancy" sign went dark. Each one-room cabin was just big enough to fit a bed and a chair, and most of the ones in back were unoccupied. There was a coffee-shop on the other side and beyond it a more modern U-shaped motel with upper and lower levels, and between both places they were able to find enough accommodation for everyone, two people to a room.

Luke waited on the bus for everyone to get off and must have fallen asleep again until Whitney came and woke him. Carl was waiting outside. He wore a sweat-shirt under his overcoat with a hood that came out of the collar so he seemed to resemble one of those monks or mountain lamas with the snow building up on his cowl and shoulders. As Luke stepped down Carl reached his gloved hand out but Luke held on to the open door while Whitney grasped his other arm. Carl told them his room-number in the other motel and said that if Luke had any problems during the night to come and get him. They both thanked him and Carl went off.

Luke couldn't really put any weight on his one leg that had gotten turned under him when he landed with the other two players on top of him. Jesus, Whiskey, Whitney says. He still has his arm through Whitney's and when he steps on that side he leans heavily against him. My knee got all swoll, Luke says, and then he laughs and looks up at his brother. Whitney's teeth even smile through the snow as he shakes his head and says, You're a fucking mess. He can feel Whitney hold up under his arm whenever he goes to step on his bad side. Tell me about it, he says.

Ever since that day two years ago when he went off by himself and somehow ended up over in Whiskey Basin which was a long ways away and then showed up at dawn the next morning with a busted hand and broken ribs but still trailing four cows and calves in front of his mare, Whitney always calls him "Whiskey" whenever just plain ol' Luke won't do.

As they go down the line of cabins to the one that's assigned to them they pass several of the team coming toward them and headed for the diner. Luke, Whitney, they say. Percy stops as Luke goes by with his head down watching the placement of his feet, and then Percy says to Whitney, Wanna nother hand? Whitney shakes his head and says, Thanks but we're OK.

Inside there's a big bed and a lamp on the nighttable beside it. Both their bags are on the floor with the football on top of Luke's, and there's a gas space-heater framed into the wall in the corner with blue and yellow flames rising upward between white ceramic cones. It's nice and warm. Home sweet home, Whitney says. He lets Luke sit in the one chair and goes into the little bathroom and then comes back with a towel that he drapes over Luke's head which is covered with melting snow. Luke bends to his boots and tries to get the first one in his hands but winces and sits back. Whitney is still standing over him and he says, Want some help? Luke shakes his head. I'll get'er, he says and looks up. Go'n eat.

Want me to bring you something? Whitney says. Luke shakes his head again. Whitney kneels down and takes Luke's boot in his hands. Hold on, he says. Luke grasps the arms of the chair and the boot comes away. Then they do the same with the other one. Whitney stands back up and says, You want some help getting undressed? Luke shakes his head. I'll be alright, he says. Thanks. You go'n eat. Whitney stands there for another moment and then steps by him with his hand on the doorknob. Last call? Luke shakes his head and Whitney opens the door and passes outside. The wind has come up hard and a swirl of flakes blows into the room as he closes the door behind him. Luke sits for another moment and then pushes himself upright. All he wants to do is lie down. He dries his head and hangs the towel on the door.

He sits on the bed and turns off the lamp and in the close darkness the flames in the grate seem bluer and almost golden as they play on his face and rise up the wall like the ghostly silhouettes of leaves flowing upward and then across the low ceiling too. He undresses slowly but his whole torso from just below his chest to his hips is bound in stiff white adhesive that feels under his hands as unsupple and precarious as an eggshell. When he finally turns to lie down, the shocking point of the blade that's under the taping seems to jab even deeper into him, and so exasperated he places the pillows behind him and gradually inches lower and lower until he is almost all the way onto his back. He didn't know when he fell asleep but Whitney hadn't returned. He dreamt that for some reason he needed to move and was instantly struck awake as if a spear had wounded him in the side and then been withdrawn lessening and lessening until he could begin to breathe again.

Somehow he had come to be on the side that wasn't hurt with a pillow propped under him. The heater had been turned down so the peaks of the flames were diminished along with the light that they produced although the phantom leaves still climbed slowly up the wall. And as if he were still dreaming but with his eyes open he sees her hand on the blanket and then feels her arm under where his head lies with her face against his shoulder and her bare legs warm and wrapped around his. She didn't say anything at all while he slowly tried to turn himself, but it was like moving something awkward and unwieldy because he had to constantly mind the axis of the knife-point that was fixed inside him so as not to disturb its precious balance.

Finally he had come far enough so he could see her eyes watching him, with his hand against her stomach under the grey team t-shirt that was all she wore. He didn't say anything either and they lay like that with their mouths together. Quickening. And then his hand rose to her breasts so sharp and hard as to wound the soft flesh of his palm by the very magnitude of their delicacy, their hard risen nipples almost seeming to catch in his skin. And the shadowy leaves still rushing upward but pounding and pounding as if some heartlike furnace now drove them. Up. He lay against her risen against the flesh of her thigh a blind wishing yearning thing vulnerable and unprotected and for her to take or turn away.

And then when she would let him be or make him go with her bent knee upraised and inward leaning and steadfast enough in its closed posture so she needn't say or do anything else to stay him, something all the way down in the well of the muscle or more truly in the hunger of the soul something seemed to release and let go and so fearful and guarded no more and all yeasaying and without even a whisper all of her said come inside me where it is safe and warm come inside me where it is warm and safe inside me, and so scalding melting fusing he was all at once lost to the cold and lost to the dark and lost to the blade of pain the fear of grief, the i-am that stands alone and apart suddenly amazed become we-two we-too and then the be-in-me.

Because however the psyche would hide behind its almost unbearable fragility, the soul is like a flower open- ing inviting, the soul is like a sun freeing the tightly closed bud to finally blossom. And so the warmth would ultimately best the cold not in duration perhaps for only the cold is everlasting, but for having been. Because love however temporal however fleeting would scar forever the iron cosmos of ice and darkness and make it forever after vulnerable and so forever after wary too because however improbable however long it takes it still could come again. The light that for having been still is. The absence growing even more powerful than the presence. And so out of the cold the chance that the warmth could come again. And love. And so maybe even love.

He watched her face until she opened her eyes watching him while she touched the bright hard taping that was wound about him as if it was a strange exotic skin that she sought to know. He rested his weight on his elbows and knees but with the core of him still up against her still yearning and for her to do with what she wished. As insistent and relentless as youth waiting and waiting and as certain as youth is too, unfolding evolving and so sloughing off childhood forever like that first skin one was born and then grew in until writhing free at last one finds oneself already clothed in a new skin, still marked with all those early scars and imperfections of course, but after that first one like a shell that had become too confining has already been cast aside. And even though the child lives on aged and maybe even hidden away all the way into death, one's childhood is gone. Irretrievably.

Does it hurt? she whispered. He shook his head watching her eyes. Waiting. And then her lips without meaning to and without warning suddenly parted and surprising even herself she laughed outright joyous, and clapping her hand over her mouth making him laugh too. But even before he could make a sound the dagger-blade under his bandaging made his eyes close and his lips part too but on clenched teeth that failed to contain his breath.

Don't, she cried. Please. With her fingers straining against the walls of his forearms as if she would try to hold the thing back that tore at him. Until finally his hands opened that had clutched both her shoulders with such a ferocity that it almost frightened her, his having grasped her as an animal might importuning only a release from its pain. And then it was gone, that pain. And as if her hands had a will of their own they drew him down again carefully drawing against the hard unfeeling adhesive that covered him. Don't, she sobbed into his chest. Please. And then drawing him down even further he was inside her once again. He was safe inside her once again. And where she still held him even as they slept.

Something seemed to be scratching at the wall where the heater was and where the leaves still slowly rose up, as if something with metal claws was trying to find a way to get in from the outside. Something metallic scraping against a like surface metal on metal with quick repetitive strokes. And then whatever it was it thudded against that same wall which was opposite the bed but still only a few feet away, as if if the sharp determined scraping wouldn't work then perhaps a more blunt assault would. Then the scratching resumed until it thudded against the wall once again. And then it was gone. But Luke had already fallen asleep again and so his dreaming mind had already made what had disturbed it a new part of his dream.

He was still asleep when she moved out from under

where he lay, careful not to wake him. She covered him anew with the blankets and then increased the setting on the heater so the flames grew brighter and gave off more warmth. And then she dressed. When she went outside she pulled the bottom of her wool cap into the high collar of her coat and then stepped around to where she thought she'd heard something scraping at the outer wall and then a heavy thud which she remembered is what had woken her, but she couldn't see anything in the dark and the blowing snow swirled in her face so she had to bow her head. A single stroke from a tiny bell suddenly sounded once and then again, much too delicate a thing quavering and then silenced in the wind. She looked up to find its source but quickly had to look down again to shield her eyes.

There was a closed service-station across the road from the motel office with a great white disk with a dark star in its center on top of a tall stanchion, and in the midst of the storm it seemed a distant moonlike thing reflecting its pale light in all the ambient and nearly co-hered snowfall. They had heard the bell before and Luke had finally decided that it was probably the air hose that hung against the outside wall, and that it must have blown off its holder. And so when the wind blew against it with enough force and at just the right angle the indicator bell that tolled the pounds-per-inch of forced air would ring. Which it did once again.

There were several big prints in the drifted snow and as she went back along the line of ragged dark shapes that were other cabins, she tried to walk in what must have been someone's nearly filled boot-holes but she also had to step between them so whoever made them took one step for every two of hers. But then they crossed over to the opposite line of cabins before she came to the one where she stayed. She heard the bell again muted and then crystal-clear and then suddenly cut off in the roar of the wind as she closed the door behind her. Her roommate lay in exactly the same position as when she had left, with her hands still clasped before her face as if she were trying to hide from something while she slept. The little travel-clock on the nightstand read five minutes past five. And nothing was the same. And yet everything was.

When Luke opened his eyes it was early in the morning. And she was gone. By the time Whitney returned, Luke was up and dressed and sitting in the chair reading. Whitney had a bag of breakfast food for both of them, and they were supposed to be back on the bus in a little more than an hour. The snow had stopped falling awhile ago and the low sky is as white as all the rest of the earth and a great stillness envelops everything, as if the storm had worn itself out with the night and now morning waited breathlessly to see what would follow.

The cold feels good to him after the closeness of the cabin as Luke waits outside for Whitney to collect their belongings and repack their travelbags. And as he stands there marveling at the world and feeling at the same time as frail as a wounded bird under his parka, the touch of her that's almost unbearable confined so to his thinking mind makes him remember almost forgetting where each of them ended in the dark and the other one began. And all of it mixed up with her hands and her lips and her hair and those phantom leaves flowing endlessly upward that he could still see if but only inside him.

And then thankfully he remarks to himself a big hole in the snow, a large bootprint on the other side of the door. And then he sees two smaller ones as narrow as a deer's going off in the opposite direction. And then another of those larger ones along the side wall where the snow is all stomped down. And up above just the outlet to the vent from the gas space-heater inside, a little metal plate set high up in the wall with a small round orifice. And so he fails to see the shiny new scars inside its collar which have been recently scored by a knife-blade.

Whitney doesn't ask him about anything except how he's feeling, but on the bus later as they're flying along the highway and homeward bound at last, Luke says that he heard something strange in the middle of the night like maybe something metal scraping against something else that was metal too. And then whatever it was it seemed to thud against the wall until it must have gone away or else he just went back to sleep again. Or both. And then this morning there're all these bootprints in the snow next to that same wall. Big ones.

Whitney looks up from his reading with some interest and then looks down again without saying anything. They both have schoolwork to do and they're both quiet until finally Luke shuts his book on his knees and closes his eyes. Moments pass in the constant humming of the wheels and then Whitney turns to him and says, You remember that old man in East Lewiston? In the paper? When they found him in his trailer? Luke opens his eyes and halfway turns his head and says, What? And Whitney says, In that big storm. When they found him they said the snow had filled in the opening to the outside vent for his space-heater was how he died. The exhaust had gotten all caked over with snow they said, and he just never woke up. He never even knew it. He just never woke up. And Luke says, Yeah I remember that.

Well, that heater in our cabin it just reminded me, Whitney says. I's sleeping on the floor in Percy and Lewis's cabin and I musta dreamed about it or somethin. And Luke is looking at him. It musta woke me up. What? Luke says. That dream. And it kept bothering me so I couldn't go back to sleep. Until finally I just had to get up. And when I come back her bootprints that remind me of a doe's somehow that go up to the door that I saw before when they were fresh are near filled in, but there aren't any new ones going the other way and so I figure she's still there. Which made me kinda glad, I have to say. And Whitney gives him that big Whitney-smile of his that never fails to make Luke feel good, even when it just comes to his mind sometimes.

Anyway, I got my knife out. The ones Lonny gave us when we were little? Luke says. And Whitney nods his head. I got mine too, Luke says. Anyway, I know it's crazy, Whitney says. I mean the odds of something like that happening again are probably a million to one. But I keep thinking, what if? What if? It was still snowing real good and I could just reach that little hole up in the wall, that little orifice from the heater, when I get all the way up on my toes. I couldn't see up that high but I could still get the blade of my pocketknife into it.

Anyway, my foot went out from under me when I

fell into the wall with my shoulder, but then I got my knife up there again just to be sure. Until I slipped again, which was when I give that wall another good shot just for good measure. And by then the side of my face that catches the wind makes me feel like I'm a damn snowman or somethin because my ear's all filled up with snow too. And I remember thinking, just like that little hole in the wall coulda been.

Whitney twists around to get his bandanna out of his back pocket and blows his nose. With gusto. Neither of them says anything. Luke looks out the window and watches the highway go by as Whitney resumes his reading. Luke rubs his eye and then shakes his head and mumbles something to himself but just barely out loud. And Whitney looks up and turns and says, What? Luke shakes his head again and says, Nothing. And then he turns and looks down at Whitney's open book that rests on his knees and says, I just said "Brothers." Whitney nods and then as a little smile starts he says, Right to the end. And then he says it too, Brothers. And turns the page. And Luke nods to himself and goes back to looking out the window.

And the snow that had begun again earlier has finally stopped altogether and he can see where the sun which is still hidden behind the overcast is almost getting ready to break through. But before it does his eyes close again and this time his chin drops on his chest and his shoulder slumps into the sidewall. Whitney turns and smiles again and then goes back to his reading.

And a moment later sunlight suddenly beams in their window following the bus and touching Whitney's open hand that lies on his book and touching Luke too where he rests his head, sound asleep at last and almost home.

YET STILL
OF THE HEART

It had been snowing since sometime during the night. Spencer stopped at the little bunkhouse that Luke had moved into when Whitney left for the university down in Colorado. He was having to attend some cattlemen's meeting or some such in Cheyenne. The radio says it slackens off somewhere this side of Casper, Spencer says, so I should be back by nightfall I reckon.

I told Mrs. Bowman I'd come by, Luke says. Toebowman's birthday or somethin. Well, tell her to set up another plate then, Spencer says. You were already invited, Luke says. Spencer shakes his head and says, I plumb forgot. And then raising his free hand as he opens and closes the door behind him, he goes to his pickup.

Luke watches him out the window as his taillights disappear behind the heavy ragged fringe of the snowfall before he even gets as far as the first cattleguard. He places another stick of firewood in the little woodstove and finishes getting dressed. He darned near just woke up and he's already hungry, he thinks. After he gets something to eat he'll go feed. Red and Aggie were off to see their new grandbaby, so the cattle will be impatient with him for his having to get to them by himself. Especially after the first load for he'll be later than they'll be expecting it but he'll still be there.

He walks over to the big house instead of going across to Red's where he'd normally get his breakfast. Spencer had left the light on outside the pantry door and as Luke trudges toward it through the dark snow he sees himself as a little boy still in his pajamas and saying Mama can I have something that he doesn't remember what and she turns with her fair hair fallen on both sides of her face while she bends over Lemon who is just full-grown then and smiling up at her with closed eyes as she rubs his thick neck saying Lemon Lemon don't you be an ol' kitchen-dog and rocking him toward that same door with his toenails sliding on the floor and both of them

Elizabeth and Lemon knowing that she'll invariably change her mind and let him stay before she ever gets as far as opening it for him. I'm coming honey she says still kneading at Lemon's shoulders as if she can't quite make herself quit like those good-luck dogs on Chinese amulets, but this one a full-fledged member of their immediate family who is gazing back at her with absolute and unabashed love.

It's already snowed more than a foot since last night. He removes his boots using the old jack that one of the hay-hands had made long before he can remember by welding together several discarded horseshoes. Ever since he was small the kitchen always seems at least half-empty. Spencer could have the whole damn hay crew in with all their kids and their wives fixing dinner for the end of another season and to him, and he imagined to Spencer too, no matter how much commotion there was it was still always mostly empty-seeming because it was still missing Elizabeth, the one person who most belonged there.

He stood at the counter eating from the pot of cold spaghetti and sauce that Spencer had cooked up the night before until he'd made a good dent in what had been left over accompanied by a couple of slices of bread and a big glass of orange-juice. It took him most of the morning to feed and then into the afternoon to reload the hay sleds. They were using the two lower hay corrals all the way across the south meadow which was under how much snow he didn't know but enough so it surely wouldn't see the light of day for probably another three months at the soonest. After he'd returned to the house again to have his lunch from the same cold pot where he'd fed at for breakfast he went down to the barn to trim Lefty's feet and then Copper's who'd had their shoes removed after the first bad storm at the start of October when the cold had set in strong enough so they knew that the snow was there to stay.

Tom and Jerry the two Belgian drafthorses that he'd used that morning were still playing with the last of their hay and he gave them each another measure of grain so that they swung back to their troughs as soon as they heard it plash against the worn bitten wood. The other and younger team of Buck and Buddy stood dreaming in their stalls as the snow continued all through the day and into the night again like a great shaggy wall of dark cold feathers patiently sifting down and filling all the high country at the foot of what someone a long time ago had renamed the Neversummer Mountains.

Luke rode Lefty the four miles or so up to the Bowmans' for he hadn't been exercised since the day before.

The snow had backed off some but when they left to go home it was coming down again heavier than ever and Luke could see when his eyes got used to the darkness where Lefty's hoofprints from earlier in the evening were all filled in and no more than shallow dimples in the otherwise unbroken surface that as they got more than halfway disappeared altogether. The wind had picked up smartly too driving the snow into their faces and making him ride with his head lowered. He had always wondered how the snow sometimes seemed to possess a barely perceptible netherlight of its own, for even in the dark he could still see if not beyond him into his surroundings then at least that diminishing flaw where he knew the road was somewhere beneath them.

Spencer had phoned from Cheyenne to extend Toebowman his best wishes and also to have him tell Luke that they had closed the roads north and west out of the city and so he'd try it again in the morning. When Luke went to get his coat Mrs. Bowman had followed after him with Bradley right behind her, and she says, Luke, you leave that hanging right where it is. And Luke says, Ma'm? And she says, There's beds aplenty and you'll still be back in time to feed in the morning. Then she turns and says to Bradley, who was Luke and Whitney's age, Whyn't you go and see if Lefty's got everything he needs.

And Bradley reaches over for his own coat though still in his stocking feet.

Luke says, We're fine, Mrs. Bowman. Honest. She peers at him with that stern look behind her glasses and her hands on her hips and her mouth set hard as if a scolding was just beginning to brew, her being the closest thing to a mother both geographically and probably otherwise that he and Whitney had known for all those years since Elizabeth died when they were little. And once or twice a week, week after week and month after month and year in and year out, leaving a casserole of food or a pan of cake or whatever with Doris at the post office to give to whichever of the Davises that came in first. And if she'd hear from Doris too most likely that one of them hadn't been out front for the school bus she always seemed to reappear, having gotten all her own taken care of, like some birdlike angel of grace with keen eyes behind her eyeglasses and kind hands rapping on the window of the pantry door until someone would come to open it and to take the covered platter from her so she could bend over and kick herself out of her galoshes which she never seemed to have the time to snap all the way shut.

We'll be fine, Mrs. Bowman. Honest, he says again. She steps in front of him and puts her small determined hand on the sleeve of his coat, that old sheepskin that had already seen better days when Spencer was a younger man but that had so much of his history worn into it and then of each of his boys who wore it in their turn at least to do their chores in, that it would probably remain a part of the physical assets of the ranch like the land and the buildings for the duration.

It's stormin somethin awful out, she says, and even your paw . . . Yes'm, Luke says bowing his head. And you know hell'd freeze over and thaw before they kept Spencer Davis from going anywhere he'd had his mind set on. Luke nods and grins in spite of himself and says, If me and Lefty don't know that road by now between your kitchen and barn and ours . . . Then he half-turns to meet Bradley's eyes which somehow convey both agreement and disapprobation all at the same time, until she pulls at Luke's arm so he looks back around.

Luke Davis, if you go off and get lost . . . No'm, he says, we're fine. Honest. She shakes her head slowly from side to side with her eyes and her lips already softening so he can see that the scolding that was just getting up steam has all but dissipated and probably even been forgotten. You boys, she says. All of you. And your paws too, still shaking her head. But Luke can see now that she's mostly just keeping herself from actually smiling, sort of like when you need to go ahead and yawn but decide to try to keep your mouth shut. Well alright, she says, but you promise me if it's too bad you'll turn around and get back here. Ma'm, he says nodding his head.

And then Bradley beginning to unbutton his coat says, As long as he's with Lefty. Maybe there's two or three Luke Davises somewheres out there in the world or their equivalent, although I shudder to think it, but there's only one Lefty. Mrs. Bowman turns and slaps at her youngest son's arm that's still in its coat sleeve. You hush, she says, with that little mock scowl she has up between her eyebrows which is also just this side of a smile. You come back now Luke, she says. You hear me? And he turns at the door and says, If'n it's too bad, Mrs. Bowman, I promise.

When they got over to the other side of the ridge the wind was much worse, as if it hadn't been all that interested in going all the way up and over the hill because it was so busy on the Davis side that it might as well leave the Bowmans for another time. And they could count on it. They all could. And so when he and Lefty started down he knew he was two and a half miles from Doris's and then another three-quarters of a mile from the ranch road that went along the bluff on the far side of the creek for nearly another mile before it finally turned in where it crossed the culvert and headed up toward their barn, which was a little more than another half-mile beyond.

He figured it must have been well past midnight when they crossed the creek which was no more than a depression in the smooth even surface of the snow between either banking. Lefty whinnied as they started up toward the indistinguishable shapes of the buildings made ghostly somehow by the nearly submerged glow of the light that shone down from the peak of the barn. He whinnied again either to proclaim how glad he was to finally be back home or perhaps just to let his stablemates know that he was on the way, although the heavy blanket of falling snow muffled his call so they seemed to step through and then beyond it even before it was lost in the wind.

Luke dismounted outside the sliding-door, wheeling and stepping down out of the near stirrup. His legs were like wooden posts that he planted in the snow or like shadows of the limbs that he assumed were still there even if he couldn't quite feel them. He dropped the reins and Lefty stood beside him with his head lowered. His mane was all knotted with ice and there was a scant line of it above each of his brows. Luke patted him against his chest. The door was frozen in its track. A long-handled shovel rested against the outer wall for just such an eventuality and he cleared away the drifted snow, baring the concrete footing and then wedging the shovel under the bottom of the door until it broke free. It was actually only frozen where the ice off the ridge of the roof melted down, the animal-heat inside making the rafters an immeasurable degree or two warmer and thus somehow aiding in the formation of the icicles that hung like an armament of great jagged daggers and swords glinting silver when there was moonlight and building drop by drop whenever the low winter sun managed to show itself.

He slid the door back just wide enough for them to enter and turned on the light, stopping outside Lefty's stall which was the second one in. The first stall was empty. He removed Lefty's bridle and exchanged it for his halter which he fastened about his head and then dropped the leadrope over the tie-rail. He patted Lefty again and undid the breast-strap and both cinches, catching the far stirrup onto the horn and lifting the saddle off him. He held it against his hip with his left hand and brought it into the tackroom just beginning to feel his legs again although not as far down as his feet just yet as he clicked on the light inside. He positioned the saddle on its wall mount and then removing his hat he knocked it free of ice and snow and hung it on the door-knob.

The wind blew snow in through the partly open sliding-door but he'd only be a few minutes and so he let it stay. He remembered the vat of cold spaghetti that had one more feeding left in it and he anticipated taking care of that bit of business before he finally went back to his own place to lie down. He lifted away Lefty's saddle-blankets with the steam rising off the horse's back and took them with his bridle into the tackroom and then turned off the light. He used the scraper to dissipate the moisture where the saddle-pads had set and then a hoof-pick to clean the snow that was still balled up under Lefty's feet. Then he went over him with his left hand fixed to a rubber currycomb and his right hand to a soft body-brush, each working in concert with the other, his left hand coming first followed closely by his right.

He mucked out Lefty's stall from earlier in the day using a wheelbarrow to take away the waste and then proceeded down the other runway where they kept fresh shavings in a great wooden bin. He wondered when Spencer might get back as he wheeled the clean bedding toward Lefty who stood with the open stall-door be-tween them. He could see Lefty's lowered head facing the bars of his stall as if he was beginning to doze off although he couldn't see the horse's eyes as he approached.

Someone years ago had fashioned a hood out of sheet-metal with wedged supports on either side to more or less protect the opening to the barn, and it was always intended that some spring after the snow was gone such a makeshift structure be made a more sturdy and permanent part of the roof. But having always fulfilled its function every winter, when the time for maintenance and repairs came which was usually after calving and before the start of haying, it never seemed enough of a priority to actually get done. The chores and tasks were endless and something that worked and wasn't broken could easily be forgotten from one year to the next.

There was so much snow, and ice under the snow, that finally breaking away from higher up on the roof from its own growing weight and beginning to slide, when it all collided with the ice and snow that was already built up on the metal hood one of the supports that was anchored against the outer wall buckled at last after all those years and the whole thing came crashing down, exploding like a booming reverberant thunderclap against the concrete footing where the outside door ran.

Lefty swung his head pulling the leadrope free and

with the open stall-door barring his way further into the barn he leapt at the partially open sliding-door, hitting its leading edge with his right shoulder and knocking it up and back as he disappeared into the night. As if being blocked from fleeing away from danger, the only other possibility was to go towards it and hopefully get past.

Luke flung the wheelbarrow aside and flew through the door shouting, Ho! Ho! The wind stung his face and blinded him with frozen snow as he tried to run into the fresh evenly spaced holes where the snow on the ground had just been kicked apart. He tried to shield his eyes with one hand but the blowing snow was so fierce that his gesture did him no good. He pitched forward face-first and hands out when his boot struck something hard and fixed under the surface and then rose back up with his hands on his thighs while he gulped in great drafts of air. He was already wet and cold as the wind buffeted off his shoulders and drove into his chest, and when he tried to run again impeded by the depth of the snow he effected a kind of uneven lunging stride with his arms sawing out to either side.

He was nearly down to the culvert and across the creek where Lefty could either turn toward Doris's and Lime Creek Road which would put him in the public way going west toward the Bowmans' or east toward

Lewiston which was a considerable distance, or he could turn the other way where the road ran parallel to the creek and along the fenceline of the lower hay meadow for miles until it eventually climbed above the ranch and through the gate that separated the private from the government lands. Or he could go directly across the road where another track wound its way back to the base of a steep cliff that rose up and eventually fell back to form another humpbacked ridge.

In geologic time Lime Creek may have been what yet remained of the great prehistoric river that carved the valley after the mountains had risen up and cooled and begun to draw the snow. Or even before that perhaps just another inconsequential underwater rift in the floor of the ocean that once covered all the land. He and Whitney couldn't find a way to visualize that even when they studied the artist's renderings in their schoolbooks. But then one day they found a tiny white paper-thin mollusc shell in the grass up from the bank when the creek was at its highest and loudest in the early summer from the mountains' runoff that filled up all the creeks in all that country. And eventually running downhill they all joined to make a river that ran into other rivers that finally flowing together too cut through whole territories until it reached the ocean at last. That they had never seen.

Other rivers. And the sea. And the Sea of Elizabeth that Spencer had told them about when he used to watch her sometimes coming up from his chores and seeing her sitting on the front steps with the soft summer wind of evening just lifting her hair as she waited for him. And with that faraway look on her face he said, as if she were listening. Listening to that inland sea washing up and falling back and washing up again with the muffled tide-like stroke of her own intimate pulse. Lapping at the edge of the meadow and washing up against the lowest step below the porch like a phantom sea that only she could hear for it lived inside her. And now they had a sign to validate her vision, spiral-shaped and hollow and where a tiny marine creature once lived. And when the world was a much younger place too.

He stood in the narrow open space that was the road across from where the bed of the creek was buried but he couldn't find any disturbance in the flat unbroken surface of the snow. He turned and tried to look behind him where he had come realizing even without being able to see into the wind that he must have missed where Lefty had turned off somewhere between the last cattleguard and the culvert. When he looked up he could just barely perceive that subtle alteration in the far darkness that had to be the light above the facing of the barn. Then he turned again and walked several steps up the road but the snow there was also undisturbed. He returned to where he'd been standing across from the culvert and walked several steps in the opposite direction toward Doris's but the ground-snow was still unremarkable.

Finally he tried to see toward the wall of the cliff across the road but the heavy shroud of falling and blowing snow hid everything. One momentary flaw made him almost hesitate but the wind came back in his eyes and he had to look down again. But he knew even before he looked up that the shadow or whatever it was stood where the timber backed up to the base of the cliff and so it would probably be when he could see more clearly just the nearest tree standing like a ghost in the darkness before being swallowed up once again.

He walked across the road with the wind swirling in his face. When he looked up he could see that same tree and then not see it. The snow underfoot was deep and unscarred and the wind raced across its surface. And then for a moment the wind fell and he could see. The tree moved. But he couldn't be sure. Like an apparition detaching itself from the dark shapes behind it and then rejoining them.

He fixed his eyes there, taking close careful steps so he wouldn't lose his balance and having to catch himself lose sight of where the thing seemed to appear and then disappear. But he knew what it was. He knew when it first made him look again even though he couldn't know then what he was seeing. Before seeing.

It was coming towards him. Very slowly it seemed although he couldn't really gauge its pace, for the distance between them seemed as constant as if they were both fixed in a tableau that afforded neither of them depth nor dimension. Like the black dot that doesn't seem to move on the horizon where the pinnacle of railway track disappears until the train suddenly crashes past you, shaking the earth and all at once eclipsing the whole blue enormity of the sky.

Lefty walked toward him taking a step and seeming to hesitate before taking another as if he couldn't yet be sure of what the stationary form was that stood before him upright and solitary and clothed too in that same chaotic cloak of blowing snow that alternately obscured the horse's vision and then finally let him see. He stepped tentatively almost recognizing it for what it was and then losing it again. But he already knew too, and before seeing too, even before it emerged once more like a lone unbending tree not tall and with both its arms against its sides.

And whatever the mechanism of the will that propels the beast—the heart, the adrenals, the old wolf fear, the old grandfather whose slashing hooves were its last defense—his knees began to come high up his chest and high under his belly, dancing like the grandfather like the wolf whose rage to live would keep it alive. And still advancing so he almost bounces on his feet, he draws a bead on the figure that stands before him caked up and down with snow and beyond whom is release and that instinctive myth of flight and freedom that is born in all living things. Then his high prancing knees began to rock him up and back cantering slowly at first when he still questioned what obstacle stood in his path and then knowing, loping and then actually running toward it, the ancient blood fury reborn fearless in his heart and all his grandfathers leaping under his throat and filling his chest so he suddenly cried out like a proclamation like a warning and then charged, driving with all his force off his hind legs and with his forefeet hardly touching the ground.

Luke didn't move. He watched the horse beginning to lope and then gallop toward him and then when the animal was close enough to see his face and his eyes he heard his voice shout something a sound before words as he threw his arms out to either side. As if he would be the barrier to stop the horse's flight. As if his pitiful hands could reach across the canyon or restrain the wind or catch the curling wave before it hurled him back against the earth. There was nothing else for him to do. The horse would either know him and the blood bond that joined them or sundered and still exultant in the ancient blood heir to and driven by then ride him down. The dull quick concussion no more than if the animal were to pass through the grasping but powerless branches of a tree and then out again, spirit brother to the wind.

Lefty shrieked again as he charged with his eyes wide and glaring and at the last moment before he would run over Luke he slid on his hind legs so that as he slowed and then planted himself he reared up with his front hooves flailing the air. And as Luke finally broke his stance, flinging himself to one side, the horse's near fore-leg came down over his shoulder. Before thinking Luke spun and springing up from the snow with that same ancient blood rage he drove his shoulder into the horse's front so the greater beast screamed again, backing and lifting off its forelegs once more. But this time the lesser beast locked its arms around the horse's neck so when Lefty began to rise, Luke's weight made him alter his intention and he suddenly just stopped as if the old blood had all at once been shut off and sent back like the stuff of unremembered dreams. And so he just stood there resting equably on all four legs.

Luke's face was crushed against the animal's shoulder so he could taste the salt and horse-reek in his mouth and feel the nicker in the horse's neck without his actually hearing it. Then his arms released and he slumped down in the snow. The leadrope that was still attached to the halter had become wound over Lefty's back but Luke didn't reach to take it up. Nor did the animal step away. He just stood there with his face lifted while Luke sat in the snow with his shoulder leaning against the horse's leg.

Without looking up the numb fingers of Luke's hand closed around the warmer skin above the animal's hoof. Lefty's full name was Left Hand Man. He was named for the sacred marking that spread over his left hip, a man's left handprint, the tips of the four fingers and the thumb. Lefty's great-grandfather some five generations back was Old Painter, one of the breeding stallions of the Nez Perce. When a mare was pregnant, the medicineman would pray over a special paint he had mixed and then immersing his fingers he would place his thumb on the mare's hip bone with his fingers spread. If the foal was born with the five finger-spots on its hip it would be given to the chief, who in his wisdom would know that that animal was indeed the chief's chief.

Spencer had given him Lefty when both Luke and the horse were young, but almost from the first Luke had understood that if he could make himself worthy he belonged to the animal and not the other way around. He had traced Lefty's lineage for a school project and then had kept reading about the Nez Perce and Chief Joseph and about the government policy that was intent on relocating the native peoples when their lands became desirable and then of course necessary.

The Nez Perce bred their horses for strength and stamina and for their temperament too. When the Whiteman came, they named that breed for the valley in the Northwest where those animals and those people lived. In peace. Until the Whiteman came. And then the Nez Perce had reason to give their animals a new name. Horse of the Iron Heart.

Fleeing from the government's four-hundred-troop cavalry of "manifest destiny" across Idaho and down the Bitterroot and back up through central Montana toward the Canadian border and sanctuary, with less than forty miles to go after being pursued for nearly four months and more than seventeen hundred miles and starving and freezing in an early October blizzard, with nothing left to sustain them they nicked the artery that was close to the surface of the skin inside their horses' ankles and

---

survived at the end on their animals' blood until the tiny wounds closed over. And until their chief, Joseph, finally surrendered so that what was left of his people still might live.

Luke and Lefty stayed as they were for what seemed a long time with the wind still keening and the snow still building on Lefty's back and on Luke's shoulders and arms. When he finally rose up he had begun to shake all over, his whole skin it seemed quivering inside his heavy wet clothing. Lefty stood to let him mount and then walked back to the drifted road and over the crossing where the buried creek still ran. Luke held on to both sides of the horse's neck while the blowing snow filled in the spaces between his fingers.

He didn't know why he was crying but the shivering flesh of his chest down his arms and across his back was not simply from the cold but also from some depthless grief sourced not only in the confrontation they had just quit but somewhere else and in a different and lost time too. Unborn wings that never would fly. And yet he thought. Something. Some thing. But he didn't know enough nor imagined he ever would to know what it could be. And all the while the wind still keened over the horse's guileless face and keened over the crown of the man's bowed head. And yet it said. And yet.

Something had turned in him that he could not have identified even if he had been conscious of it, some change or shift that he wasn't even aware of, some un-named alteration that turned something in his soul so he was never again to see with the same eyes nor feel with the same hands. A shift of such infinitesimal subtlety and yet of such absolute thoroughness that he would bear its cast for as long as he took in the light, for as long as he processed the cold.

He was still a boy, in a man's body perhaps, but still a boy when he promised Mrs. Bowman to return in the storm. But that instant of rage and grief when he knelt and sprang forward instead of back—to somehow save himself by leaping at the thing that could destroy him rather than trying to avoid it—then he became no longer the boy who said he would return if the storm got too bad but instead something even previous to the boy, something grown from the boy both forward in vision and back. Not back to what is lost to time because noth-ing is ever lost, but back toward the source, back to the very wellspring where earth and breath divide, this the clay and the stone and this the breath and the blood and no wiseman to determine that one or the other is more or less. And all of it, broken and whole, unspeakable sor-row. All of it, sundered and joined, unspeakable joy.

When he crouched under the horse's leg whose hoof

like fate's perfect cudgel would break him and leave him in the long snowy night freezing all previous sense and will and even right being, when instead of flinging himself away to avoid the rock the hammer of the next hoof and like the beast even lacking the choice to do so and leapt forward embracing the thing that would dash the breath out of him, that instinct that acts even before the mind can choose would determine the whole rest of his life. Where something even deeper than the marrow knows that the cost of avoiding what one fears is even greater than the actual object of that fear and so the fear itself is even more corrosive even more destructive than all the frightening potential of the thing that arouses it.

Luke leaned even lower, resting his chest on the crest of Lefty's neck, the frozen hair of the horse's mane both harsh and comforting against his lips and his arms encircling that broad flat muscle to either side so his hands which were warm at last lay against the horse's throat. The reiving indefatigable cold and yet the strong slow throb of the horse's pulse and against it small though insistent too like a tiny quiet thread alongside the wonderful drumming torrent his own heartbeat lesser and greater and yet still of the heart. And yet still of the heart.

with grateful acknowledgment

Milton M. Adess
Chip Ridky, D.V.M.
Dan Lott

Eleanor Jackson
Kate Medina

ABOUT THE AUTHOR

JOE HENRY received his MFA from the University of
Iowa Writers' Workshop, but he attributes much of his
learning to his many years as a laborer, rancher and
professional athlete. A renowned lyricist, he has had
his words performed on more than a hundred record-
ings by artists ranging from Frank Sinatra and John
Denver to Garth Brooks and Rascal Flatts. In addition to his many music awards, Henry also received
a National Conservation Achievement Award from
the National Wildlife Federation "for the celebration
of the natural world in his work" and the Colorado
Governor's Award for Excellence in the Arts. This is
his first work of fiction.

ABOUT THE TYPE

This book was set in Requiem, a typeface designed by the Hoefler Type Foundry. It is a typeface inspired by inscriptional capitals in Ludovico Vicentino degli Arrighi's 1523 writing manual, *Il modo de temperare le penne*. An original lowercase, a set of figures, and an italic in the "chancery" style that Arrighi helped popularize were created to make this adaptation of a classical design into a complete font family.